Finding Christmas

Seth Sjostrom

wolfprint, LLC
Camas, WA, 98607

This book is a work of fiction. Names, characters, places, and incidents are products of the author's imagination or are used fictitiously. Any resemblance to actual events or locales or persons living or dead is entirely coincidental.

For information, contact wolfprintMedia.

Library of Congress Control Number (LLCN) 2012944228

Trade Paperback
ISBN-13: 978-0-9854389-4-4
ISBN-10: 0985438932

Hardcover
ISBN-13: 978-0-9854389-3-7
ISBN-10: 0985438940

1.Josh Daniels (Fictitious character)-Fiction. 2.Romance-Holiday-Commerical- - Fiction.

Second wolfprintMedia Digital edition 2020. wolfprintMedia is a trademark of wolfprintMedia, LLC.

For information regarding bulk purchases, please contact wolfprintMedia, LLC, at wolfprint@hotmail.com.

United States of America

for my sister, Tonya

my eternal inspiration, Hayden

Acknowledgements

Deepest thanks to my family – Tom, Linda, Steve, Wende, Brady, Tonya, Chaney, Koen, Coreena and Jamie for your inspiration and all things family.

For Kathy, Ethan, Logan, and Kiara for love and life after heartache.

To Michelle and Lorna for keen eyes and keeping myself and my characters straight.

To John Eley for cover photos.

To Hayden, my unyielding inspiration.

Finding Christmas

Chapter One

Josh paced the length of the lanai, taking a deep breath as he listened to the very one-sided phone conversation. Taking his eyes off of the magnificent backdrop of the Pacific Ocean, he glanced at his watch. "Mom...Mom, I have to get down to see my next group of customers."

"Please just tell me you'll think about it," his Mom pleaded.

"I'd love to, I really would, but I have to work. Everyone else has families…it just makes sense. Maybe I'll come back for Easter. "

"What about your family? Josh, you haven't been home in nearly three years," his mother continued to make her case, "Besides, I know you hate putting Kaya on that plane all by herself."

"It kills me," Josh admitted.

"Then at least you'll get to share the adventure of travel with her."

"Fine, I'll think about it, Mom. I have to go. I'll call you later," with an exasperated sigh, Josh slammed his phone shut. Clasping his hands around the rail, he watched several sets roll in off of the Pacific and crash against the rocky shore. Shaking off the frustration of the conversation, he psyched himself up for his sales presentation.

Less than forty-five minutes after bounding into the presentation room of the Kona, Hawaii vacation timeshare resort, Josh burst into the business office beaming. "Sharon, my dear, just closed my second deal of the day – a two-bedroom, two weeks a year!" he placed the folder in front of his assistant.

"Nice job! You haven't lost your December touch," checking the clock Sharon added, "And it is only eleven A.M."

"Now I can pick Kaya up early," he grinned, snatching his keys off of his desk.

"She will love that."

The young office receptionist walked by, flashing a friendly smile at Josh, "Have you pulled your Secret Santa off the tree for the party?"

Josh froze with his hand on the door handle, turning to face the spirited girl. His mouth parted, though no words came out. The look across his face said that he was trying to measure his response. Sharon broke in with a wink, "I'll handle it. You get Kaya." Appearing relieved, he slipped out of the office without another word.

"What did I say?" the receptionist asked, a bewildered look spread across her face.

"Josh doesn't celebrate Christmas," Sharon replied.

"What do you mean he doesn't celebrate Christmas?"

"Ever since he moved here from the mainland, he just has rejected Christmas. He buys his daughter a present each year, but that is about it," Sharon shrugged, "I think sending Kaya to her mom's each year just brings him down too much."

"That's so sad. He's such a nice guy."

"I know. As soon as Josh puts Kaya on the plane, he has a personality change until the day she comes home. He becomes a workaholic; I end up with a pile of closings when I get back," Sharon sighed, "This year, it sounds like his Mom finally talked him into flying home while Kaya is with his ex."

"Good for him," the receptionist declared and then thoughtfully added, "Good for you, too!"

Pulling his open-top Jeep alongside the curb, Josh jumped out. The hundredth time this year, he picked his daughter up from school, and it was the hundredth time he was excited, a smile spread wide across his face. Waving to the office staff, Josh waited for the period to be over so he could intercept Kaya while classes changed. Leaning against the wall, he joined two mothers who were also waiting to pick up their children early. One of them gave Josh a quick smile.

Checking his watch, he waited impatiently for the bell to ring. When it finally did, he scanned the crowd of primary school children for the second-grade class. Hordes of children streamed into the hallways on their way to lunch, forcing Josh to crane his neck.

Recognizing a few of Kaya's classmates, his focus sharpened on the happy faces until he saw the one he was looking for. Kaya was oblivious, giggling with one of her friends, skipping along to her next class. Her wispy curls bouncing as she walked, Josh loved seeing her so content, innocent. Each day he picked her up from school was like opening a favorite gift – exciting, complete joy surrounding his heart.

"Kaya…," he called out.

Hearing her father's voice, she instantly broke from her conversation and perked her head up. Seeing him, she grinned and ran towards him, "Daddy!"

Bracing himself, he readied for the imminent launch, Kaya leaping into his arms. Looking up, she frowned, "You're here early."

"I know. I wanted to spend some time with you before our trip. Make sure you have everything you need."

"Does Mrs. Jenkins know?" the second-grader asked, her voice showing her concern.

"You are so responsible. Yes, I called the office when I left the resort. I closed two deals in record time today," Josh smiled, holding his daughter's hand and gripping her backpack in his other.

"Good job, you're the best salesman down there. Sharon tells me that all the time. She also tells me she's surprised you do that job," Kaya gushed at her father.

Pushing the doors open with his back, he let Kaya scoot through and allowed a mother and her little boy to pass by. "Thank you, Josh," the mom smiled, "Oh, are you in town for Christmas? Some of us single parents are getting the kids together for a little holiday social next week."

"Oh, I'm sorry, Kaya would love that, but I am afraid we are mainland bound. Thank you, though," Josh replied.

"Oh, that's too bad, maybe some other time. Merry Christmas, Kaya!" her face displayed her disappointment before returning a final cheery smile.

Josh murmured a return greeting and gave Kaya a squeeze. His daughter grinned, looking up at her father, "She likes you, Daddy."

"Who?"

"Bobby's mom. I noticed the way she smiled at you. Besides, she was really inviting you, not me," Kaya reported, "I see ladies look at you all the time when you pick me up."

"They're probably looking at you, wondering how I had a cute as a button girl like you," Josh declared, tickling her on the ribs.

"Daddy!" Kaya squealed as she danced around, trying to avoid more tickling.

Helping her in the Jeep, he made sure she buckled and kissed her on the forehead, "Next stop, packing for the mainland."

Snapping the last latch on his suitcase, Josh plopped on the edge of his bed. He took a deep breath as he dialed his phone. He had put off this call all day. Before he could even get his thoughts in order, a voice called "hello" from the other end.

"Dana? It's Josh," he replied, "How are you doing?"

"Ready for Christmas and Kaya coming home. Your Mom says you are even making the trip this year," his ex-wife answered, surprise ringing in her voice.

"Yeah, I guess her nagging and guilt trips finally wore me down. I hate traveling over the holidays, but at least Kaya gets company," Josh said, after a long pause, he added, "Hey, since I'm coming out there, I was wondering if I could steal Kaya for a day or part of a day for Christmas."

"I don't know, Josh. We have a lot planned for her. These visits are pretty special. We don't get much time."

"I know it is a lot to ask. I couldn't help but try."

Dana sighed, "I'm sorry, Josh. I don't think so. We'll see you at the airport."

Josh tossed the phone on the bed and rubbed his hands over his face. Disappointed, he sulked through the house until he found Kaya. Slumped on an overstuffed suitcase, she was fast asleep. Smiling, he gently guided her into bed and kissed her cheek. Zipping her bag the rest of the way closed, he placed it by the door next to his own.

Chapter Two

The open-air Kailua-Kona airport overflowed with holiday travelers. Tourists and locals alike were loaded down with pineapples and boxes of chocolate-covered macadamia nuts for their mainland friends and families. Josh had already lined his suitcase with boxes he had bought at Costco for the trip. He had stuffed a couple in Kaya's bag for her to give to her mom.

Josh held onto their carry-ons as Kaya followed in step behind him. Together, they sat and waited for their flight to be called. Kaya looked up at her dad, glad that he was by her side. Inching over, she placed her head against his arm. Josh glanced down and smiled, putting his arm around her, "You'll get to see your mom in five hours."

"Five hours? That's such a long time," Kaya exclaimed and then cooed, "It won't be bad 'cause you're with me, Daddy." A tighter squeeze from Josh's arm told her that he agreed.

"I'm glad I get to travel with you. I hate when you leave," Josh admitted.

"I know," with a grin, she brightened, "But leaving always gives us a chance to be happy coming home!"

"It sure does," Josh smiled as he watched a Hawaiian Airlines jet drop below the tops of the wind ravaged palm trees on the opposite side of the runway, "That's probably our ride."

A half-hour of people watching later, their flight was called, and Kaya was gripping her father's hand as the jet roared down the runway and began to lift into the air. Josh chuckled at his daughter, noticing she had clenched her eyes shut for take-off. "That's my favorite part," he told her.

"Not mine, it's scary."

"Look, you can see shadows underwater. That one there looks like a whale," Josh pointed over Kaya's shoulder out her small window.

"Wow, the water is so beautiful from up here. You can see the coral reef," Kaya peered through her window.

"We have kayaked there. We could almost touch the spinner dolphins that day," Josh pointed to a crescent-shaped bay.

"We almost turned over when that boat went by," Kaya shivered.

"They just spiced up the trip with a few waves. Besides, even if we did capsize, you can out swim me. You would have had to save me," Josh laughed.

"Oh, Daddy, you're silly!"

As the plane distanced itself from the island and they entered the open water of the Pacific Ocean, the view became a bit more monotonous. They turned their attention to the movies that they brought. Selecting one of Kaya's favorites, Josh lifted the armrest and let Kaya lean against him as they watched the screen on his laptop. He was glad that he was making the trip, if for this alone. As he settled in to enjoy the moment, he fought to shake thoughts of the inevitable. He knew once the flight landed, he would have to let her go. Squeezing his eyes tight, banishing the notion, he kissed Kaya on the forehead and drank in the moments that they had together.

Cloud by cloud, the miles ticked by, they played games and shared snacks that Josh stowed in his bag. At one point, a flight attendant stopped to chat with them. While she spent most of her time talking to Kaya, about what grade she was in and what she wanted for the holidays, her eyes most frequently fell on Josh. As she pulled away, she put a hand on his shoulder and told them to let her know if she could make the flight more comfortable.

When the attendant was clear of earshot, Kaya giggled as she whispered, "She likes you, Daddy."

"Kaya, not every woman that stops to talk likes me. It seems it only happens when you are with me," Josh protested.

"Just think how many notice you when I'm not there," Kaya snickered.

"You're the only woman in my life. I'm fine with that."

When they reached the Portland International Airport, Josh's stomach tightened. With each step through the terminal, he wanted to stop and turn back, taking Kaya with him. Looking down at her smiling face, he could sense the excitement she was feeling to see her mother. Her sunny affect was enough to get him to swallow his selfish wishes and continue for her sake.

Slipping through the crowded choke point of security, they entered the terminal lobby. Dana and her boyfriend were front and center of the large crowd awaiting passengers for pick up. Josh's heart sank in his stomach one more time. He couldn't bear to let Kaya go, especially with her mother's new boyfriend there to whisk her away. Looking at all of the happy faces surrounding him, picking up their loved ones for the holidays, reminded Josh of exactly why he had rejected the entire season since the divorce.

Stopping short of his ex-wife, he let Kaya run up and give a hug. He watched in silence as the boyfriend was introduced, and Kaya smiled with the warmth that he knew his beautiful daughter would. Dana looked up flashed Josh a brief smile as her boyfriend collected Kaya's bags. As they turned to leave, Kaya broke from the pair and ran back to Josh. Dropping to a knee, he accepted a huge hug from his daughter.

Pulling back, Kaya looked into her father's eyes as tears filled her own, "I love you, Daddy. Merry Christmas."

Choking back his own tears, Josh managed a breathy reply, "Merry Christmas Kaya."

Reluctantly letting go, he watched his daughter jog back to her mother. Still on one knee, travelers maneuvered around him as his eyes helplessly followed his daughter through the terminal and down the escalator towards baggage claim. The sight of Kaya's blonde curls bouncing merrily away stung his heart. Sullen and defeated, he slowly made his way to his feet and shuffled out of the lobby. Not wanting to manage the awkwardness of waiting together, Josh stopped at the nearest lounge. For the first time in all of his travels, he accepted the "shot for a buck" option with his beer.

The Rose City cab pulled alongside the curb. Josh handed the driver a wrinkled assortment of bills, not really hearing the "Merry Christmas" the man murmured in broken English. Stepping on to the sidewalk, he set his bag down. Despite the cold and occasional near-miss of spray being thrown up by cars pushing through slush, he stood motionless, taking in the scene. The house was adorned with holiday décor as though it were a Thomas Kinkade scene. Wreaths hung in each window as well as the front door. Lights were strewn atop each bush and bookending conifers that flanked either side of the front door. Such was the traditional fare at his parent's home. Each holiday enveloped in perfect display – a trait he had adored growing up and had even carried into his own home until the divorce.

Now the sight just made the pit in his stomach harden into an even tighter knot.

Taking in an enormous sigh, he picked up his suitcase and made his way down the stone path to the front door. Setting his luggage down, he raised a fist to knock on the door. Before he laid his first rap, the door swung open. Josh's mother stood in the doorway with a great smile across her face as she reached her arms out to hug him. "Josh, I can't believe you're here!" her songbird tone suddenly switched to a much more stern inflection that Josh had heard all too often growing up, "Why didn't you call? We were going to pick you up!"

"I know, Mom. I didn't want to make you guys come out. The airport was crazy."

"Did you get Kaya off okay?"

"Yes," Josh muttered curtly and snatched his bags from the porch. Before he could even set his luggage down again, he was smothered with waist-high hugs from his niece and nephew.

When the sea of children abated, Josh was met by the rest of his family. His father offered his usual stoic greeting and then whirled away to grab his son a cocktail, fulfilling his host duties. His sister was last in line. She hugged him tightly, pulling away, she looked at him intently, "I am so glad you made it Joshy."

"Come on, Josh, let's get your things to your room," Josh's mother called, leading him down the hallway.

Josh knew where he was headed. The den where the "single" visitors stayed, as it had only a pull-out bed and was the room without a bath attached. "You'll be in here. I hope you don't mind. Amy and Bob have the guest bedroom, and we put the kids in the game room upstairs, it is so cute, they lined all of their sleeping bags under the pool table," his mother giggled.

"It's fine, Mom."

"Well, put your stuff down and let's get back to the living room, everyone has been waiting for you, especially your nieces and nephews."

"I will," Josh agreed, plopping his bags alongside the sofa, "Just give me a couple of minutes to shake off the jetlag."

"Okay, but hurry up!"

As his mother left, Josh's eyes flitted around the room. He had never spent a night in this room. When he was with Dana, they either got the guestroom, or they just drove from home five miles away. The room seemed as cold as the weathered brown leather sofa that was to be his bed. The realization that he was spending the holidays in full swing with his family made his head reel. Sitting on the arm of the couch, he looked at his unpacked bags and wondered if it was too late to turn back. Vigorously rubbing his face, he felt that he made a big mistake by making the trip.

He longed for the islands where the holiday season is far less obvious other than a slight uptick of tourists. Something about palm trees, sunshine, and Santas wearing board shorts and Hawaiian print shirts made ignoring the season that much easier. He wished he had work to bury himself in, working every possible shift and collapsing at home or surfing until he couldn't paddle another stroke. Staying active and preoccupied allowed him to make it through with minimal trauma. Here, Christmas was all around him. His mother had even placed a small plastic tree in the room, decked with many of the ornaments he had made as a boy.

The sounds of Bing Crosby crooning "White Christmas" and kids giggling as they shook presents under the tree made his reluctance to join his family even stronger. He loved spending time with them, but Christmas was just too hard without his daughter. Hearing his dad calling for him with a freshly brewed "Tom and Jerry", he knew he could not put his presence off any longer. Lifting himself off of the sofa, he followed the sounds down the hall.

"There he is! It isn't Christmas 'till you've had your first Tom and Jerry," his father said in his hearty voice, "Glad you're here, son."

Accepting the mug of holiday libation, Josh managed a slight smile, "Thanks, Dad."

"You know, you being here means a lot to your mother. You've made her Christmas."

"I'm glad. You know it's not the family I avoid…"

"I know, Son. I know," his father replied softly.

Chapter Three

The Daniels' home rang with the sounds of Christmas preparations. Josh's mother and sister were processing dozens of sugar cookies from bowl to pan to the table for the kids to begin decorating. Sarah and Noah circled the house, each holding a decoration reindeer, helping them fly from room to room. As they made their way through the house, they belted out Christmas carols in tune with the CD that was playing.

Each song brought back so many memories for Josh. He tried to focus on the recollections from childhood, but his Christmases with Dana and Kaya kept coming into the forefront. He remembered playing the very same CD as they decorated their tree. It was their last full year together as a family. He had no idea at the time there would not be another to follow. His thoughts jumped to the last Christmas on the mainland before he and Kaya moved to Kona. His divorce from Dana was finalized over that holiday. The ideal family and life that he thought he had shattered that cold December like an icicle set free from a rooftop.

Now his family was Kaya, every day, Josh spent with her was his Christmas. He celebrated every day back home with his daughter, never missing a school event, playing with her every day, having special dinners together. To those who observed him, he was an ideal father – though he didn't realize it, was well thought of by the women in the school PTA. For Josh, he felt as though he couldn't do enough for his daughter. After the divorce, Josh focused on two things – Kaya and work, as long as work did not interfere with his daughter's needs.

Josh smiled at his nephew, who was holding a ratty stuffed Rudolph. He had been chasing his sister who danced a snow monster along the floor, but paused to look up at his uncle. "Uncle Josh, will you play with us?"

"Of course I will, Noah," Josh kneeled on the floor next to the kids, "What do you want me to be?"

"You can be Santa Clause," his young niece Sara replied, handing him a toy Santa.

"Yeah, you'd make a great Santa, you give the best presents!" Noah agreed, and then swept his Rudolph next to the snow monster, "Now let's get her!"

Finding a break in the action, his parents in the kitchen making preparations for dinner and his sister and brother-in-law had the kids washing up for dinner, Josh slipped out of the house.

Sloshing through the snow in a pair of his father's galoshes, he found solace in the backyard. The gray clouds overheard hinted towards more snowfall. Josh didn't mind. He always liked the snow. Pulling his cell phone out of his pocket, he dialed Dana, hoping to speak to Kaya, but when he reached his ex-wife's voicemail, he snapped his phone shut.

Not ready to return to the pre-Christmas festivities, he plopped on the snow-covered seat of a swingset. It was the same swing that he and his sister Amy played on as kids. His dad had repainted it and suspended new seats from fresh chains for the grandkids. Admiring the gentle snow-covered slopes of the backyard, he pushed himself around in a tight circle.

"You know, you'd go further if you actually lifted your foot off the ground."

Josh turned to find his sister grinning at him, two uncapped beers in her hands. "I knew I would find you out here. Avoiding the holiday brouhaha?"

Accepting one of the beers, he offered the snow-covered seat next to him.

"My butt is going to get wet!" Amy protested in mock disgust.

"When did that ever stop you?" Josh asked, taking a swallow of beer, "Remember when we were kids? We would play in the snow until our lips were blue, and Mom would have to bundle up to come out and chase us inside."

"We had a lot of fun growing up. Even if you were a twerp of a little brother."

"Aw c'mon, I wasn't that bad…"

"You were alright, especially when you let me dress you up in my doll clothes," Amy laughed.

"Let you? I couldn't even walk or talk yet!"

"Oh yeah, I thought you went along with it pretty easily," Amy smiled, "So. How are you, little brother? And not the Christmas card "things are fine stuff" you give to Mom, give me the straight scoop."

"Things are fine. My job is going well. I get lots of time with Kaya. We live in paradise…what else is there?" Josh shrugged.

"You are a great father, but what about you and your needs. You can do better than timeshare sales for starters. Didn't you talk to that Marketing firm in Honolulu?"

"I did. Corporate nine to five, travel, clients at night…my gig at the resort allows me to be a dad. I make pretty good money. Long as I make my numbers, they let me come and go as I need. By the way, if you and Bob are interested, we have some terrific deals going on," Josh grinned.

"We don't need a timeshare; we have family in the islands."

"Touché," Josh cheered his sister's bottle, "When are you guys going to make it out?"

"Hoping my stocking has a couple of airline tickets this year," Amy winked, and looked at the path through the snow they made to the swings, "Kind of tough being here without Kaya, huh?"

"It's the worst."

"This used to be your favorite time of year. Your Christmases were so awesome; even Mom agreed to have it at your house. Your place was better than the Griswold's, heck you were the Griswolds."

"Didn't do it alone," Josh replied simply, moving his eyes from his sister to the ground.

"You and Dana made a good team – created one heck of an amazing daughter. But then you were a wonderful, dynamic person before you married her," Amy said sternly, and then teased, "How is the love life on the island? Lots of bikini-clad tourists…"

"Nah, I have enough between work and Kaya."

"Josh, it's been almost three years. It's time to get back in the game, little brother."

"I don't know. It just doesn't feel right," Josh admitted, "Not because of Dana or anything, but for Kaya."

"What doesn't feel right? Are you worried about Kaya being offended by you spending time with another adult? Or a woman? When you guys were visiting for Spring Break last year, she would pick out girls for you as we walked through the mall. She is worried that you are missing part of your life."

"I am not unhappy. I love my life with Kaya. I feel good about myself. I appreciate the concern, Sis, but…"

"Relax little brother; I am not going to grill you. I am just glad you came; I know Mom and the kids were excited that you would be here. If you need, I'll help deflect any of that untoward Christmas spirit that comes your way," Amy winked, "Now come on, we'd better get back in before your disappearance is discovered."

The talk at the dinner table consisted of questions about life in Hawaii, how Kaya was fairing in school, and thankfully for Josh, deflected to how his brother-in-law Bob's dental practice was growing and where his parents were traveling in the New Year. Josh's false confidence had been increasing as he thought that he had successfully avoided most of his mother's doting.

"Are you seeing anybody, Josh?" his mother asked.

"What?" Josh choked, "No. I've just been enjoying being active for Kaya."

"What about friends? Have you made any since you moved to the island?" his mother continued.

Josh played with the food on his plate, "I have friends, Mom."

"I just worry about you. I know you are a great father to Kaya, but you need to make time for yourself too. It can't be easy being a single father," his mother pressed.

"Carol! Leave the boy alone. He won't ever come back if he constantly has to defend his life," his father scolded.

"I'm proud of you, Josh, I just imagine it has to be very difficult," Josh's mother conceded.

"I know I have my hands full, and I have Mom, Dad, and Bob to help out. I don't know how you do it, but you have done a fantastic job with Kaya," Amy chimed in.

Josh put his fork down and looked around the table at his family, a determined demeanor cast over his face. "Being a single dad to Kaya isn't a burden, it's a blessing. Being able to spend so much focused time with her, being a part of her school, her life…I feel incredibly fortunate. She and I are a family. Sure I would have given anything to keep us together as a family with Dana, but as things turned out, I couldn't ask for anything more. I love my life with Kaya.

I don't do a whole lot outside of work and Kaya. But she's my best friend, and I am okay with that. So don't pity me because I'm a single day, envy me because I get to experience being a parent in ways that most men don't."

A harsh quiet fell over the table, save for the occasional stray clink of silverware against a dinner plate. Bob broke the silence, "I envy you."

Amy smacked her husband on the arm, "You want to be a single dad?"

"Of course not, he's just inspired me to make time with a kids a greater priority than the practice," Bob choked in defense.

"Humph!" Amy grunted, casting her husband a suspicious glare.

"I didn't mean to stir up a hornets' nest, I just get concerned about you and the load you carry," Carol retracted.

"I know, Mom. I'm not upset; I just want people to realize I like my life with Kaya. It's simple, it's Aloha, but it's filled with love. I couldn't ask for more," Josh conceded.

Amy shot Bob another stern glare, "You better talk with that much passion about me!"

Bob grinned as he poured more gravy on his potatoes, "Would you settle for me talking that way about Sarah and Noah?"

Whatever tension had built around the table was released in a chorus of laughter. Josh was the most relieved when his life ceased being the topic of conversation. As he looked around the table, he did feel as though there was an enormous empty space. It was the first dinner during the holidays that he had attended without Dana. But it was the absence of the spunky eight-year-old that truly created the void.

As Josh's mind wandered back into the conversation at the table, he studies his niece and nephew. He missed seeing them grow up and wished he were more a part of their lives. Nudging his bother-in-law, he urged them to make a trip to the islands for a visit. He even threw out that maybe the entire family could make the trip. The offer met with mixed reviews, with the exception of the kids who were all over the idea.

Josh offered to Noah and Sarah that when they made it to the island, he and Kaya would teach them to surf. Playing in the waves was one of his and Kaya's favorite pastimes. No matter how crazy life seemed to get, the power of the ocean never failed to get his heart and mind back on track. The two kids giggled at the idea, especially when Amy suggested Bob give it a try too. Seeing his sister and brother-in-law interact and laugh with their kids was bittersweet for Josh. While he was proud of his sister for creating such a wonderful happy family, yet it made him miss Kaya even more. The truth was, he did avoid the holidays. Without Kaya, they just didn't matter.

When each belly at the table reached capacity, Nicholas suggested that the family adjourn to the living room to watch holiday movies. Josh demanded that his mother join the rest of the family while he cleaned up after dinner. The solitude and menial labor sounded sweetly therapeutic to him. As he scrubbed dishes and placed them in the dishwasher, he smiled when the occasional laugh or squeal erupted from Noah and Sarah. Josh pictured the scenes from the movie unfold as the sounds flowed into the kitchen, intermingled with the chorus of his family's laughter. He couldn't count the number of times he had watched each animated holiday movie as a kid and then re-watched with Kaya after she was born.

As he mindlessly circled a plate with the dishrag, he noticed more snow had begun to fall outside. While he and Kaya would occasionally play in the snow atop Mauna Kea, it wasn't the same as it was here. Snow in the winter and leaves falling in autumn were two of only a few mainland things that he missed.

When he finished with the last dish, Josh snuck through the hallway, trying to avoid the family room. He paused as he crept past in the hall, peeking at the all too familiar movie playing, a favorite he used to watch every year with Dana and Kaya. The power of nostalgia at Christmas was one of the unbearable things that made him avoid the holiday altogether. Successfully circumventing the family, he plopped down into his dad's overstuffed leather chair. His eyes settling in on the rows of bookcases lining the wall. The bottom row was an endless line of photo albums.

Pulling one from the shelf, he set the book in his lap and began letting the pages fall open. The album started with the entire family traipsing through a pumpkin patch, one of their favorite annual rituals. A picture of Dana smiling at the camera, her amber hair blowing in the breeze and the fall sun lighting her face, revealing her faint freckles...Josh zeroed in on Dana's smile. There was so much captured in such a brief moment. Her smiles were always one of life's wonders – amazingly beautiful, soulful, yet filled with a sense of mischief. Josh's love for her was unrivaled until Kaya was born. He thought that his life was perfect. That Halloween was the year before things fell apart. As Josh flipped through the pages, he remembered how good things were, how complete he felt.

The next page had a picture of Kaya riding atop his shoulders amidst a sea of brilliant orange pumpkins. His daughter was the one constant that remained positive in his life. His greatest ambition each day was to find ways to make her laugh, to make her life as good as it could be. The following pages took him through Thanksgiving, Amy and Bob's annual holiday.

Finally, Christmas. The pictures hit Josh with a wave of memories. He loved Christmas with Dana and Kaya so much. It was a wonderful time of year for them. They held parties for their friends, took Kaya to see Santa Clause, and embarked on their yearly romp through the woods to find the perfect tree. He and Kaya would spend hours analyzing hundreds of candidates, until Dana would finally tire of the search and demand they pick one. Josh would let Kaya make a few swipes with the saw to help cut the tree down.

Back at home, Dana was in her element. Humming to Dean Martin as she produced cookies and eggnog as she handed took her spot kneeling beside half a dozen boxes of decorations. She would hand her husband and daughter ornaments one by one, directing them where on the tree they needed to go. All of her efforts and tyrannical decorating paid off, overseeing a stunning holiday tree.

Their entire house was magical at Christmas, from the smells of fresh evergreen, the warm décor, to the ambiance of an endless supply of carols played on the stereo. Evenings were spent as a family in front of the fireplace playing board games before cuddling on the couch to watch movies. Kaya would fall asleep beside them as Dana and Josh enjoyed stolen moments together.

Josh traced a photo of the three of them posing in front of their tree, the happy family. Josh sighed as he sipped from his wineglass. He still had no idea where that happy family had gone. The following year he had made a job change to spend less time traveling. When he returned from his final trip, he somehow felt that things weren't the same. A few months later, he and Dana were sleeping in separate rooms in the house. Two months after that, in the middle of the Christmas season, their divorce had entered the finalization stages.

Since Dana had returned to school, she okayed Josh to have primary custody of Kaya. When he faced a layoff that same year, he discussed taking a job in Hawaii. Thinking she might move to Hawaii at a later point, too, she agreed, not knowing her business at home was going to blossom so quickly. Many painful arguments later, their current arrangement was settled. A month in the summer, winter break, and Spring Break were Dana's. Josh enjoyed custody of Kaya the rest of the year.

The last picture in the album was of Josh and Kaya playing on the floor with her new pretend oven. He remembered the building anticipation that took hold of his daughter as Christmas came closer. Most of all, he remembered the complete joy that filled Kaya until she finally collapsed in exhaustion. He would carry her sleeping body to bed, sliding a new stuffed animal under the covers beside her.

Sliding the book back in its place, Josh took one more sip of wine before he leaned back into the chair. He closed his eyes, letting the movies that were playing in his mind affect their sweet torture on him until he fell asleep.

Chapter Four

Josh had awakened with tremendous trepidation. He knew that was the day of his family's shopping trip. Hours of grueling endurance amidst throngs of shoppers, some hasty and pushy, others wandering aimlessly with their loved ones, soaking in all the romanticism the holiday had to offer – neither sat atop Josh's list of people he wanted to spend his time. His reluctance grew more fervent when his mother insisted that he ride with her and his dad. Amy winked at her brother from her family SUV as both vehicles pulled away from the driveway.

The trip to the shopping center was as excruciating as Josh had assumed it would be. The ride began with his parents singing to carols along with the radio, occasionally urging Josh to join in. In between holiday songs, his parents broke into the prerequisite argument about which route to take to the mall. Once there, the secondary dispute about where to park and his father's grumbling about the crowded lot did nothing to improve Josh's outlook on the day.

Trudging through the slush, the Daniels family avoided the soaking wake from drivers searching for their own parking spaces. The unpleasant elements actually made Josh welcome the warm and dry sanctuary of the mall. A sentiment that melted away immediately as the first of many shopping bag burdened inhabitants slammed into him without so much as an "excuse me". Seeing the cross look on her son's face, Josh's mom chided, "Come on, Josh, it's the holidays, peace on earth…goodwill."

Sighing, Josh wrapped his mom's shoulders with his arms, "That it is, Mom. That it is."

"So, what should we hit first? Josh, do you have any shopping to do?" Nicholas asked as he studied the mall map, with Sarah pointing her finger to the "You are here" star.

"No, Dad. I ordered some stuff online before I left, it should all arrive in a day or two."

"Shopping island-style, I suppose," Josh's dad remarked.

"Better than trying to get it on a plane," Josh shrugged.

"Well, I guess it is divide and conquer," Nicholas declared, clapping his hands together as though he were a quarterback ready to call a play.

"Let's just start at Macy's and see where we go from there," Amy suggested, knowing her brother did not want to be isolated with either parent. They would drag him from store to store, line to line regaling him with the triviality of life, or bombard him with questions about his life.

Somehow, the entire family managed to negotiate the torrent of shoppers milling in each direction of the concourse. Pouring into the Macy's anchor store, the crew took in all of the holiday décor and displays of random items that impulse shoppers might add to their bundle. Josh focused on Noah and Sarah, asking them about how good they have been for Santa and what they hoped to receive for Christmas. Amy threw a smile at her brother's way; her two kids always followed Josh around like puppies when he visited.

"Josh, mind if I steal them? I think I would value their opinion on what to get their uncle," Amy asked.

"Hmm, I do value Sarah and Noah's opinion. Alright, but Bob gets veto power, okay?" Josh feigned, weighing the decision and released his hug on the two kids.

"Josh, you can come with us. Your father and I are looking for what to get your aunts and uncles," Josh's mother piped in.

Sarah and Noah were healthy distractions for Josh, if his parents exchanged views on presents as they did the car ride over, that was a conversion he did not want to make. "Yeah, how about I catch up with you guys Mom, I have a few last-minute things I want to look for."

"Oh, maybe we can help…," his mother added.

"Maybe they're for you and Dad," Josh replied, raising a discerning eyebrow.

"Oh, okay. We'll be in the housewares section, and then we are going to head to the book store," Carol declared.

"Okay, be right behind you," Josh returned with a half-hearted promise.

As the family parted in three directions, Josh made a beeline out of the store. Unsure of where he wanted to retreat to, he looked both directions down the concourse. He found the chaos of the mall courtyard extremely overwhelming, driving him blindly forward. Swiftly moving towards an exit, he passed a chain restaurant. His eyes caught a bank of televisions above a long rack of glasses. He knew instantly that he had found his refuge. Slipping through a stampede of shoppers, he made his way into the restaurant. Waving off the hostess, he found a place of solace relative to the rest of the mall.

Sliding into a barstool, he felt the stress of the day melt away. Selecting a microbrew on tap from the bartender, Josh stared at the football scores trailing across the bottom of the screens. As a frosty mug slid in front of him, he took a big gulp of the amber liquid. Letting out a big sigh, he relaxed against the back of the barstool.

"Escape from the family?" a beleaguered looking man, cupping a near-empty beer mug asked.

"Huh?" Josh looked up, not expecting someone to be speaking to him, "Oh, yeah."

"It's brutal out there. I'm sucked into it each year. I barely liked it when I had my kids with me. Since the divorce my family uses extortion and guilt most years to get me to come," the man shared solemnly and nodded at the bartender who pointed at his now empty glass.

"Guess I'm in the same boat. Wouldn't mind if I had my daughter…"

"Yeah, the kids really make the holiday. I get them the day after Christmas this year. They got used to it. I think they make out pretty good with two Christmases," the man replied thoughtfully and took a swig of his fresh poured beer, a froth mustache lining his lip momentarily. "I'm Bob."

Josh shook the man's hand, "Josh. I am lucky enough to have Kaya most of the year, so Christmas is kind of forfeited for me."

"Good and bad, I guess. Holidays must suck…" Bob paused, realizing how brutal his choice of words was, "Aw, I'm sorry. Didn't mean that to come out so harsh."

"No worries, you're right. They do. I usually work through the season, but my family begged me to visit," Josh admitted.

"Isn't that the way. They mean well, but we would just as soon be left alone."

Nodding, Josh agreed, "It's just worse to be drug out to watch whole families together, doing all the things that we used to do for Christmas."

"Ain't that the truth," Bob swallowed another gulp of beer, "Josh, cheers. And Merry Christmas…or Bah Humbug…either way hang in there. Good for you to be with your kid most of the rest of the time. A sacrifice I guess I might make if I could."

"Cheers to you. Merry Christmas is fine. I don't wish to take away Christmas from anyone else; I just don't need it anymore."

"Little brother!" a disapproving voice called sternly from behind Josh's barstool. Josh spun to find his sister standing behind him. Her grin belying her faux anger. "We wondered where you had snuck off. Bob ratted you out. He said this is where he'd have gone."

"Sorry, Sis," Josh shrugged sheepishly.

"Don't be sorry, just order me a beer," Amy grinned, "Who's your friend?"

"Bob," Josh's bar mate smiled, sticking out his hand, "You must be the extorting family member."

"I am. But I am on my brother's side," Amy grinned, slipping into a barstool beside Josh and introduced herself. "Extorting family member, huh?"

"His words, not mine," Josh said over his beer.

"What is it for you, Bob? Mother, sister…?"

"And the nieces and nephews," Bob admitted.

"Any other members of the Grinch club?" Amy asked. She laughed as her rhetorical question was met by three other men in nearby stools raising their hands. Reaching for her beer, she polled the men for their scenarios, each quite similar to Bob and Josh's.

Soon, the whole bar was launched into the challenges of Christmas, the quiet, sullen group of escaped men now laughing and sharing experiences. Amy was startled when a voice rose from behind her, "Young lady, you were sent to retrieve Josh, not join him."

In exaggerated shame, Amy pretended to hide her beer glass behind Bob's, "Sorry, Dad."

"Don't be sorry, just order me a beer," Nicholas demanded.

"How'd you know we were here?"Amy asked.

"Your husband went turncoat to save himself. He said this is where he'd be if he were Josh. And then he said this is where he'd be if he were you looking for Josh. And before he could ask your mother and me to keep an eye on Sarah and Noah, I volunteered to come find you both myself," their dad grinned, accepting a freshly poured beer from Josh.

"I can't believe you three," Josh's mother fumed as she passed out the eggnog, "Especially you Nicholas, shame on you. Bob, the kids, and I wandered around for half an hour looking for you."

"Goose chase?" Josh whispered to his brother-in-law, who nodded. "Thanks!"

The Daniels matriarch was not finished with her rant, "And that was a half-hour after Amy was supposed to be searching. And who knows how long Josh was cavorting in that bar. We were Christmas shopping as a family!"

"Well, Mother, we're all here now. The kids are ready to decorate the tree…and this eggnog, it is really good. Did you do something different to it?" Josh's father took charge, distracting his wife back into the holiday frame.

"Well, I did shave fresh nutmeg, that makes it pop, doesn't it?"

"Let's go and bring in those tubs of tree decorations," Bob suggested to Josh, further supporting his father-in-law's bid to change the subject, "They're in the garage, right?"

By the time the two men hauled in the last tub, Josh's mother had slipped back into Mrs. Clause mode, busily stringing lights on the tree while humming to Nat King Cole. Once the first strand had been wound to the top, Carol let Noah and Sarah wrap the next set by dancing around the tree like a maypole. As they circled the tree, the two children giggled the entire circuit.

Settling into the corner of the sofa, Josh enjoyed watching the kids play. One by one, their grandmother handed them an ornament, frequently directing them where on the tree they should be placed. Josh laughed as only about half of the time, the kids complied. Before long, the bottom half of the tree was trimmed to perfection, with the exception of the top remaining noticeably bare.

"Josh, you want to help with the taller parts of the tree?" his mother asked, holding out a crystal angel.

Agreeing, Josh took the angel and began placing it on a limb. "This alright, Mom, or would you like it somewhere specific?"

"That's fine," Carol replied, ignoring the fact that her son was teasing her direction over the children, "Oh, this one is so cute." She pulled a delicate reindeer from the tub.

Josh reached for the ornament. It was a simple, handmade clay Rudolph. The reindeer's antlers were different sizes, and the red nose sat slightly askew. Josh looked at it like it was a long lost masterpiece. He remembered Kaya coming home from school the last day before Christmas break. She could barely say hello before handing it to her Dad. Josh remembered that she almost looked nervous in anticipation as he pulled away the tissue paper and revealed the little ornament. "It's Rudolph, Daddy! We watched that the night before art class. When teacher let us decide what to make, I wanted something for you for Christmas," Kaya had squealed.

Staring at the ornament now, his daughter miles away with her mother, Josh fought back his emotions. Instead, he simply took the box it had been stored in and gently replaced it. "I think I'll hold on to this one, Mom."

For a moment, his family sat very still and quiet, not knowing how they should respond. Breaking the silence, Bob jumped to offer his services to finish trimming the tree, allowing a relieved Josh slunk to the back of the room. Receiving a pat on the shoulder from Amy, Josh decided to retreat to his room for a few moments. He did not want to pull down the mood of the rest of the family. Once in the solitude of the den, Josh sat on the pull-out bed and re-opened the box. He studied the decoration Rudolph intently, loving each line that Kaya's fingers created. Every flaw was a beautiful reminder that his daughter had crafted the lopsided reindeer herself. In several spots, her fingerprint could be clearly seen, it's tight looping circles captured in the brown clay.

Choking back the tears that were ruthlessly welling from within, Josh once more put the ornament back in its lonely home. He felt guilty that the sounds of laughter rising above the carols sung by Burl Ives made him hurt even more. Feeling it best for everyone, he decided to sneak out of the house while the family remained engrossed in the festivity of decorating.

Passing his father in the hallway, Josh knew his clean escape had been foiled, Nicholas eyeing the jacket he had tucked under his arm. Stammering, Josh offered to run to the store to replenish the rapidly consumed eggnog for the family. Understanding the real reason behind the trip, Nicholas acquiesced and suggested his son take his all-wheel-drive sedan. Thanking his father, Josh slipped into the garage, avoiding passing through the living room, and what he knew would be his mother's insistence that the eggnog could wait until the next day.

Removing the freshest layer of snow from the windshield of his father's car, Josh climbed in and backed out of the driveway. Pleased with the relatively clean getaway, Josh admitted, with his father's help, a growing feeling of relief washed over him. Just getting away and driving aimlessly through the snow-blanketed neighborhoods was refreshing for him. He knew that the visit was going to be hard on him, but he hadn't thought about the heaviness his mood might impose on the rest of the family, Sarah and Noah in particular.

Navigating the slushy roads, Josh found himself in a neighborhood all too familiar. Part of him urged his hands to turn the wheel down the next side street as soon as possible; another part of him could not resist continuing ahead. Passing through an intersection, he found himself stopping in front of a small craftsman home.

Pulling alongside the curb, Josh admired the snowman in the yard. Wrapped in a bright red scarf, the round figure wore a crooked smile made from rocks pressed into his snowy face. Josh chuckled, thinking that he would have made the snowman ten yards to the right, because he knew from there, you would be able to enjoy the creation from the living room window. His eyes moved to that very window. Through the frosty panes, he could see the family inside, putting the finishing touches on their tree. The father stretched to get the angel atop the tree while his daughter admired it from his side.

Josh's mind entered that room, the way it was three years ago, when the photos on the walls were his. In the corner, he could picture logs aflame in the fireplace, a Christmas movie playing on the television mounted above it. In nearly the same spot as this family's, he saw himself stretching to reach the top of the tree, just as the new inhabitant had. Kaya by his side, letting him know when he had it just right. He could see Dana curled up in front of the fire, watching the two complete the family tree. He could almost smell the pine, hear Kaya giggling - he could certainly feel the warmth that those days filled within him.

The tree complete, the three of them would huddle together, listening to Christmas music, just staring at the tree for hours. Those were his favorite days. The stresses of work and to-do lists were abjectly disregarded. The only concern was which board game to pull out or which movie to watch next. As long as they were together.

Through the haze of his memories, his eyes caught a figure looking out at him. The little girl peered through the window at him in front of her house. Suddenly, the reality that he parked in front of someone else's home hit him squarely. Slipping the car into gear, he pulled away from his old house.

Once more, Josh found himself driving sans direction through his former hometown. He wasn't ready to go back to his folks' just yet. His mind was still processing the scene at the house, undecided if the mental visit back in time was more painful than it was pleasant. He did know that he felt heavier than ever. He wished he were back in Hawaii - either in the midst of a long workday, riding the swells atop his surfboard, or sitting at Huggo's cafe watching the waves roll to shore.

Passing by a coffee shop, Josh hastily turned the wheel, the tires slipping slightly through the slush-covered entry of the parking space. If not a cocktail at Huggo's, he would find solace in an eggnog latte. Stepping into the shop, he was greeted with the subconscious pleasure of coffee aroma. The warmth of the shop in contrast to the chilly air outside, the relative quiet aside from the occasional growl of the burr grinder, and the soft lighting helped Josh drift into a feeling of contentment.

The barista greeted Josh with a polite smile and holiday sentiment. With a half-hearted Merry Christmas, he placed his order. Pleasantly, the barista offered to bring his coffee when it was ready. Passing the few occupied tables, Josh found a secluded corner to hole up in. From his coffee shop induced calm, he enjoyed people watching as he waited for his beverage. He quietly observed a young couple lean across the table towards each other as they cupped their mugs of coffee. Their eyes intent on the other's as they smiled through hushed conversation.

Josh's gaze flitted to a department store Santa Clause enjoying a break. The man, looking beleaguered and tired, made Josh hope that the poor guy was finished for the day. In the corner of his eye, Josh noticed a figure heading his way. Turning his head, he was just in time to see a coffee cup sail through the air in his direction. Following the coffee was the barista who was falling through the air like a felled tree. Instinctively, Josh flung himself out of his chair, sliding across the floor on his knees. Reaching out, his arms hugged around the young woman, just before she slammed into the floor herself. The force of the impact knocked him on his back, the barista landing squarely on top of him.

For one brief moment, they lay with eyes locked, their noses inches away from the other. The shock melted quickly into embarrassed discomfort, causing them to scramble to their feet. "You okay?" Josh asked, only now noticing his pants and shirt were wet with the stain of spilled latte. Nodding, the young woman seemed to be taking stock of herself while fighting the mortified look that had washed over her face. "I'm sorry to have…tackled you. Just kind of reacted," Josh apologized.

"You're sorry? You saved me from bouncing my clumsy head on the floor. I'm sorry for nearly landing a piping hot latte…and myself in your lap," the very red-faced barista declared.

Listening to the apologetic young woman, Josh was struck by how her eyes danced when she spoke. Through her blushed cheeks, delicate freckles lightly sprayed across the bridge of her nose, pronouncing her warm smile. He couldn't help but be impressed by how she held herself, given the situation.

"Don't be sorry. It wasn't your fault. I think the slush from my shoes left a slick spot on the floor… I think we're back to me apologizing."

"These floors are slick every day, all day this time of year, it was all me," the barista pressed, looking at Josh's soiled shirt and khakis, she added, "Let me grab some towels to get you cleaned up." Spinning away, she dashed behind the bar to return with a stack of towels.

Having retrieved the cup, its contents completely spilled on the floor and his clothes, Josh handed it to the girl. Patting himself dry, he could see the very much still sickened look on the poor barista's face, "Seriously, don't worry about it. I'm glad you're okay, and besides, these were really not my favorite pair of pants anyway."

Laughing, the barista thanked him, "You're nice. Let me at least make you another cup."

"Can I pick it up at your counter this time?" Josh teased.

"Absolutely," the woman grinned behind her crimson cheeks.

Seeming relieved to slink back behind the sanctity of the espresso machine, the barista quickly produced a second latte. "And here, take a gift card, the next coffee or three are on us."

"Better than on me," Josh grinned.

"Hey…"

Launching into a broad, kind smile, Josh retracted, his hands out in front of him, "Just kidding. Have a Merry Christmas."

"You too."

Having showered and ran water on his coffee-stained clothes, Josh flopped in the study's wingback chair. Pulling out his cell phone, he scrolled through his contacts and pressed the call button.

Dana's familiar voice answered, "Hi Josh. Hope you're enjoying your family, tell them I said 'hi'."

"Of course. How is Kaya?"

"She's good. She misses you, but I think she's having fun. She's helped me make cookies and played in the snow with Roger. Even got her to sit on Santa's lap," Dana shared.

"Not too many years left of that."

"No, afraid not. I did get a copy of the picture for you."

"Thanks, I can't wait to see it," Josh replied, pausing for a moment, "Hey, I don't want to step on your time, but… do you think I could have her for a few hours one day? I know Sarah and Noah…everyone…would love to spend some time with her."

"I'm sorry, Josh, I don't think so. You have her the rest of the year. This time for me is precious; I don't want to miss one second."

"I understand. I just haven't been near her for Christmas in years..."

"I know Josh," Dana admitted softly, "I don't blame you for asking. Please don't blame me for not sacrificing the limited time that I get with her."

"I don't, Dana. I do hope you have a great time with her."

"We will. I'd have her talk to you, but she crashed on the couch while we were watching "A Wonderful Life". Why don't you call later on? You can call anytime, though she especially misses you at night."

"Thanks, Dana, I will."

"I'm so glad he came for Christmas," Carol said as the family settled into the living room.

"We all are," Amy agreed, "I hope he's doing okay. I know he has been pretty sensitive, especially for anything that reminds him of Kaya."

"Or anything that reminds him of Christmas," Nicholas added.

"I'm pretty sure aside from ordering presents online and buying some for Kaya, there is not a lot of Christmas in Josh's life," Carol chimed.

"It's too bad, remember when he was little? He was the biggest holiday geek. He would run around the house singing Christmas carols all December- long. I wanted to kill him by the fourth day of Christmas," Amy laughed.

"He and Dana were Christmas. Their house was always decked. Not sure if I found it inspiring or frustrating how good of a job he did on the lights," Bob said.

"Yeah, Christmas at their house was special. I remember Mom fought it for so long, and after she finally gave in that first year, it was all over. Dana and Josh really made everyone feel like the classic family Christmas," Amy agreed.

"It is sad. The holidays and family were such a big part of him. He just isn't the same when Kaya is gone," Nicholas sighed.

Watching Noah and Sarah on their bellies, their feet sticking up in the air as they flipped through pages of a snowman picture book, Amy envisioned loudly, "Hard to imagine what it would be like not to share the holidays with the kids. Got to be tough on him."

"You're right. As much as I wanted him here…and am glad he's here, I didn't think it would be so hard," Carol admitted.

"He'll be alright," Amy promised, "Just let him flow and don't push. He'll be alright."

When Josh rejoined the family, they had settled in for the night. Noah and Sarah were in their pajamas, soliciting a smile and hug from their uncle. The adults were either reading or working through a crossword puzzle. Sarah glanced expectantly at her uncle and then at a board game. Josh nodded and grinned, launching the kids into a frenzy of setting up game pieces.

Sliding on his belly, Josh snaked between his niece and nephew. Before too long, Josh was watching Noah's gingerbread man cross the finish line triumphantly – much to Sarah's chagrin - into the Candy Castle.

Josh glanced at the wall clock. "Excuse me, guys. I have a quick call to make."

Escaping the noises from the rest of the house, Josh retreated to the study. Dialing Dana's home number, though he realized he shouldn't have been, he was startled and somewhat disappointed when Roger answered the phone.

"Hi Josh, Merry Christmas. Let me get the phone to Kaya. She is just getting ready for bed."

Josh waited impatiently, listening to Roger tell Kaya that her dad was on the phone. With the first utterance of Kaya's sweet voice, which always squeaked a bit when she got excited, his heart radiated with overwhelming warmth. "Daddy!"

"Hi, sweetheart. I miss you."

"I miss you too, Daddy."

"Are you having fun?"

"Yep! Mom and Roger took me to see Santa Clause. I told him some stuff for you…and Mommy got you a picture."

"I know, that was nice of her. What else have you done?"

"They took me ice skating. I wasn't very good. I wish it was snowboarding, 'cause it's a lot like surfing," Kaya said excitedly.

"You would be good at that," Josh admitted, a part of him imagine the two of them were floating out past the breakers as they spoke, "I'm glad you're having a good time."

"I am. I wish I could be with you, though. You know daddy, Roger is real nice, I think you would like him. He's going to read to me tonight before I go to bed. Maybe I'll read to him. I love you, Daddy!"

"I love you too, Kaya," Josh said softly, "Have sweet dreams. I'll call you tomorrow."

As he closed the call, his heart slunk heavier than ever. He knew he should be happy that Roger was kind to her, that he should be glad for Dana for that matter. But the image of someone else building the traditions and nurturing his daughter in his stead stung at his heart as though it had been wrapped by tentacles of a thousand jellyfish.

He pressed his forehead against the window of the room, hoping the cold surface against his skin could quell the pain. Staring at the shards of moonlight slashing across the snow-covered ground, they looked like a nautical star. He wished it could give him direction. As much as he was glad to be home with his family, he couldn't help feeling as though he were alone in some distant, foreign land.

His family understood his tangled heart as best as they could, but they couldn't really understand. How could anyone? Not too very long ago, he thought that he had the perfect life. He never imagined Kaya growing up in a fractured home. Every image of the future that he had held for his little family – from Kaya's school plays, graduation, vacations together, the pictures included a doting mother and a father. Despite three years passing, the concept of being divorced from Dana was unfathomable. Josh didn't pine for her; there was just an odd void, and each day since seemed like he had been living a parallel life. Only work and Kaya made him feel in synch, whole.

Sucking in a deep breath, he left the relative serenity of the study to rejoin his family. His father's hot toddies and his wonderful nephew and niece who adored their uncle would be his solace for this cold winter night.

Chapter Five

"Are you sure you won't come with us, Josh? I think there is a box of your old ski stuff in the garage," Josh's mother asked, a tone of hope resonating loudly.

"No, you guys go on ahead. I'll catch up with you later."

"It'll be fun; Pop's has found a great hill for the kids. It even has a tow rope to get back up," Amy added.

"For Sarah and Noah, I'd love to, sis. I have a few errands I need to get done anyways," Josh replied, finality clear in his voice. He knew inside, hanging out in the cold, watching a dozen other fathers playing with their kids was not something he wanted to experience.

"Alright, Bob will have his cell phone if you change your mind."

Stepping into the foyer, he gave Noah and Sarah each a hug. Both clad in thick layers of winter clothing, so much that they waddled around like robotic penguins. Josh laughed as he waved goodbye, smiling past the final pleas from the two kids for him to go too. Their faces had almost beaten Josh, but he remained resolute and shut the entry door. With a large exhale, he conceded that he needed at least one holiday-free day.

Settling on the couch, he roamed the television channels for a football game. Nearly every station was a holiday special, each harvesting a new cascade of memories for him. Switching off the television, he sat on the couch, his chin resting on his hands. It seemed every square inch of his parent's house enveloped Christmas. Not that he could argue, his home used to trump the holiday trimming by a sizable margin. He was determined to give himself one day's worth of a holiday hiatus. As he mulled his options, his mind clued in on the one place that he felt truly content, despite its décor and traditional holiday music in the background. For whatever reason, the atmosphere of the coffee shop made him feel comfortable. Maybe it was the usual cadre of other hapless escapees searching respite. Perhaps even his misery desired company, of sorts.

Nodding to himself with his epiphany, he grabbed his coat and his father's car keys. Surfing through the stations, he found one playing the top songs of the year. Suddenly his day of escaping Christmas had traction. Even as he sped past the Salvation Army volunteers ringing their bells, the tree lots teeming with families searching for just the right evergreen, the half a dozen Santas wandering the town – he was satisfied that he headed for sanctuary.

Pulling into a parking space, he was surprised that there were relatively few cars in front of the coffee shop. Then again, a glance at his watch told him it was lunchtime, a lull between peak coffee hours. Pausing to hold the door open for two ladies exiting with steaming cups, he entered the sanctuary of the coffee shop.

Ordering his usual latte and a bag of almonds with dried fruit, Josh thanked the young man across the counter. The barista promised they would bring him his drink when it was ready. Grabbing his makeshift lunch, Josh retreated to a corner table, as he had the day prior. Aside from two ladies surrounded with shopping bags and a couple who were reviewing their gift list, the coffee shop was quiet. The Christmas music playing overhead was subtle and barely hung in the background, heard lightly wisping through the air when the grinding and frothing of the espresso machine finally fell silent.

Turning his attention to the frost lined window, Josh watched as an elderly gentleman held his arm out to assist his wife, reaching the safety of the cleared sidewalk. Josh smiled to himself as the courtesy was rarely seen these days. Lost in his thoughts and people-watching, he was startled by the figure standing at his table.

"I can't believe you came back."

Josh turned to see the attractive woman who had served him the day prior gingerly holding his latte cup out for him, "Usually when I throw steaming hot drinks at people, they're not so quick to return."

"I guess I don't scare easily."

"That or you find the help terribly entertaining," the woman grinned, "Sorry, but I promise there will not be a floor show today."

"Too bad, I may have to find another coffee shop…"

"Nope, I think you'll be a regular here. After all, if that experience didn't scare you away, I think this is the place for you," the barista laughed and then blushing, added, "I really am sorry."

"Don't worry about it," Josh waved the girl's apology off, after a few moments of uncomfortable silence, he asked, "Can I buy you a cup of coffee?"

"I should've bought yours. I am off in a few minutes, sure. Let me finish up. I'm Ashley, by the way," she agreed, holding out her hand.

Josh introduced himself and shook her hand. As he watched her walk away, he was suddenly consumed by anxiety. He asked himself what he was doing, inviting her to have coffee with him. He reconciled that he was just being kind because she was so embarrassed. Yes, he was putting the young lady at ease for her spill the other day. Suddenly uncomfortable that his quiet day at the coffee shop was now a conversation with a stranger, Josh squirmed in his seat as he tried to enjoy his latte. His mind reeled off numerous excuses why he needed to take off, but his brain failed to produce one before Ashley was sliding into the seat across from him.

"Thank you for the coffee, by the way. The house will take care of it. Is there anything we can get you? You deserve it after yesterday," Ashley offered, still obviously embarrassed by her spill.

"I promise you I am fine. Probably pretty corny asking to buy a barista a cup of coffee."

"Not at all. It was sweet of you to offer. Besides, you are helping me procrastinate. If I weren't, I'd have to tackle the books, and I have no desire right now," Ashley conceded.

"College?"

Shaking her head, Ashley replied, "Payroll. I'm not just a clumsy waitress. I own this joint!"

"Well, I like the shop. The staff is a bit shaky…." Josh teased.

"Hey, now, I thought we were over that!" Ashley rebuked in mock disdain.

Josh felt color rush to his cheeks as he squirmed, "Sorry, I couldn't resist."

"It's alright, well deserved."

"So, you own the shop?"

"Yep, this is my third year now. Never thought I'd own a coffee shop," Ashley shared.

"No?"

"I was happily making a living as a grade-school teacher. I used to stop in here all the time to grade papers when I didn't want to be alone. It was practically my second home. When the owner passed away, a developer was going to take over, and who knows what…plop in a franchise, I suppose. This place has been an institution in this town for so long. I just hated to see it go. On a whim, I cashed what pension had vested, scraped every dime I had, and bought the place."

"Wow, to take such a risk and have such conviction. That is very impressive," Josh admired.

"My friends thought I was crazy. They were probably right."

"I don't know, it seems like you've done pretty well."

"Thank you. It has been tough, but I'm glad I did it. I feel like such a part of the community," Ashley beamed, "How about you? Did you find something you loved to do?"

"Sort of. I found a job that I love what it allows me to do, spend time with my daughter," Josh replied, fidgeting and squirming now that the questions reflected towards him...

"You have a daughter?"

Beaming, Josh nodded, holding up a picture of Kaya on his phone.

"She's adorable."

"Thanks. Kaya is…amazing. So, to answer your question, I have resolved to do what I do so that I can be there for her. I sell timeshare at a resort on the big island of Hawaii."

"Ah, that explains the tan. I was going to get to that question, you don't get like that around here in December," Ashley grinned, "Were you always in sales?"

"No. I was a PR exec across the river in Portland for years. It was stressful, crazy hours…hard on a marriage. Hard to be the dad I wanted to be. So when Kaya's mother and I got a divorce, I decided to work for one of my clients. Now I live, I guess, what the locals call 'Aloha'," Josh replied, feeling the heat rise up his neck.

Sensing Josh was pulling away, Ashley comforted him, "It's okay, you don't have to…"

"It's alright. I guess I don't reach into my past too often," Josh shrugged, "For some reason, I find you easy to talk to."

Ashley's soft look of concern melted into a warm smile. Feeling encouraged, she pressed gently, "Life in Hawaii must be nice."

"It is. I work hard while Kaya is in school; otherwise, we get to surf, hike, play volleyball…"

"Sounds like you have a great relationship with your daughter."

"I do."

"She's lucky," Ashley began.

"I'm lucky," Josh corrected, his voice earnest in his response, "She is an incredible gift. I'm blessed to spend so much time with her."

"It's a great time to be back here. I love the snow, soft and bright. The ponds are frozen for skating…its Christmas paradise," Ashley said, her voice glowing to match the bright expression of her face.

"Yeah, I do miss the snow. I remember we used to hike east of here to Punch Bowl, the waterfall would freeze solid, like it was put on pause. It was breathtaking."

"It's frozen now. I had some friends who went out there last weekend. I had to mind the shop so I couldn't go," Ashley reflected for a moment, and then her face brightened, "Hey, we should go out there. Do you have plans for the day?" Subconsciously she reached out for Josh's hand as she made the suggestion.

Taken by surprise by the spontaneous gesture, Josh felt the warmth from her hands for a moment and instinctively pulled back, stumbling, "I, uh, no…I…"

"I'm sorry. That was a little forward. I just thought it sounded like it had been a while, and I could show you…"

"No, you're fine. It's just that…," Josh thought for a moment, looking into Ashley's slightly crestfallen face, "You know what, let's do it. It will be a nice afternoon."

"Great! I'll grab some waters for us, and we'll go," Ashley declared excitedly, and sprinted behind the counter, snatching a couple of waters and snacks, shoving them hurriedly into a sack. "Dan, I'll be back to help close up, and Jenna should be here any minute. Thank you!" she called, pulling her coat from the rack against the back wall.

Ashley grinned a mischievous grin at Josh, "Let's go!"

Chapter Six

For Josh, the drive to Eagle Creek induced a myriad of conflicting thoughts and feelings within him. His mind oscillated wildly between moments of panic, wondering what he was doing venturing out into the countryside with a strange woman, only to be then exorcised by Ashley's infectious smile and soft but persistent push to open him up. She lobbed light, inquisitive questions about his life in Hawaii and growing up in the tiny river town of Camas. Despite his nervousness, he found the conversation to be comfortable and relaxed.

Before long, Josh's curiosity about the alluring woman in the passenger seat led him to turn the tables as he thoughtfully crafted questions for Ashley. As she shared bits of her life, growing up in a little suburb an hour from Portland, teaching, and her bold decision to buy the coffee shop; Josh found the answers didn't impress him as much as the passion that Ashley managed to convey in almost everything she talked about. The seemingly simple coffee shop owner was an intelligent, motivated, striking woman who seemed to tackle everything she encountered with heart and conviction. With each passing mile, Josh couldn't help but to be more impressed with her.

As the breathtaking scenery flashed by their windows, Josh grew more and more at ease with his companion. She managed to extract a sense of comfort with him, making him feel as though they had known each other for years. When they paused their volley of questions at each other, they joked about their first encounter in the coffee shop. As they replayed the scene of Ashley crashing into him in slow motion, the two erupted in laughter that elicited tears.

The Columbia River Gorge, the geographical division between Oregon and Washington, was a long split in the Cascade Range. Forged by the mighty river and notorious winds, the Gorge was the epitome of the range's namesake. Waterfall after waterfall flanked the basalt walls on either side of the canyon. The winter cold tamed most of them frozen in a milky wave, seemingly motionless until the next thaw.

Piloting the car through the ascending twists and turns of the scenic highway, Josh was soon crossing the Bridge of the Gods and pulling into the Eagle Crest lot. Josh had to push the throttle to punch through the snow at the entrance. Theirs was the only car in the deserted lot. Josh paused before turning off the ignition, thinking about trudging through the snow out in the middle of nowhere. Almost sensing his hesitation, Ashley urged, "Come on! I'm sure your memory can't do this justice."

Flinging her door open, Ashley stepped out into the snow. Pulling the top button of her coat tight, she circled to the front of the car meeting Josh. "Sure about this? You don't exactly look dressed for an excursion in the woods."

"Oh, it's a short walk. I'll be fine. Besides, it's worth it," Ashley replied cheerily, tugging at Josh's sleeve.

Compelled by Ashley's exuberance, Josh fell in step with her. Almost instinctively, they leaned into each other, fending off the cold breeze that shot through the canyon. To ward off the chill, Ashley slipped her arm into Josh's to huddle even closer as they did their best to navigate the snow-covered trail. For a moment, Josh's body tensed at the contact but then relaxed, finding their linked arms strangely pleasant.

The two made their way along the path, which was delineated only by the apparent channel it cut through the trees. Each turn took the pair deeper into a wintry splendor. An even blanket of white covered everything, bowing the limbs of trees, insulating sound so that only their footsteps crunching through the snow and their breathing were heard. When they paused, the forest was silent, only the occasional sheath of ice slipping free of a limb, crashing like tiny shards of glass to the snow below. Despite the grey clouds overhead, the world was bright and radiant in the snow's reflection.

Soon, the path opened up to a clearing. Along the back edge, the hillside made a solid backdrop of white, split in the middle by cascade of ice. Hanging thirty feet from the hill's crest, the waterfall stood motionless, creating a massive playground slide made of ice. At its base, the large pool that created the clearing in the forest was a clean expanse of ice.

Turning to Josh, Ashley beamed, her bright blue eyes locking onto his, "Isn't it beautiful?"

"It's incredible. I'm glad you suggested it," Josh agreed softly, his eyes consuming the dramatic winter scene.

"I can't think of anywhere I'd rather be today. It really puts me in the Christmas spirit," Ashley cooed and once more tugged on his sleeve, "Come on. Let's go onto the ice."

Hesitant at first, Josh relented. He had quickly learned how persistent his companion could be. As he took the first tentative steps towards the frozen pond, he remembered sliding on the ice as a kid, ducking in behind the frozen waterfall. It was indeed a natural wonder. Josh supported Ashley as they gingerly made their way down the embankment. They cautiously the tested the edge of the ice, Josh poked at it with a large stick and then pressed down with one foot before committing. Once satisfied, Ashley twirled her way to the center of the pond. Josh watched from the edge, playfully nudging pinecone with his stick like they were makeshift hockey pucks.

Josh couldn't help but to be captivated by the sight, the brilliance of the snow and ice-filled bowl, flanked by white trees and the centerpiece waterfall, Ashley looked like a snow princess in her long, white coat, twirling like a figure skater on the ice. Josh admired her childlike zeal as she slid along the ice. Her long chestnut hair and wind-kissed cheeks stood out against the sea of white. Ashley paused in her skating to smile back at Josh, watching him mindlessly dribble the makeshift puck back and forth.

As he stood on the surface of the pond, the clumsy, perky barista suddenly struck him in a very different way. In the center of the ice, stood a beautiful, striking woman. The notion took Josh by complete surprise, his face, his body as frozen as the waterfall. Helpless, he was lost in the image that danced along the ice before him. The world seemed to stop for a moment, as if allowing Josh to notice the beauty that was right in front of him. The beauty that had been with him all day. Suddenly feeling as though he were gawking, he clumsily shot the pinecone puck across the ice, sliding it between a pair of boulders.

"Nice shot," Ashley called, bringing the divine image that had taken Josh back to life. Skating his direction, she asked, "Are you gonna hang there all day, or are you going to venture away from the edge? It's solid." Grasping his hand, she led him further out onto the pond.

Sliding his feet along the surface as though he were wearing skates, Josh took the lead. Grasping Ashley's hand, he swept them to the edge of the waterfall. Guiding her gently, they tucked in behind the icy cascade.

"It's like a frozen palace," Ashley whispered, her voice echoing softly in the icy cavern. Light radiated through the translucent walls, making them glow a brilliant blue. The silence in the ice cocoon was both eerie and ethereal. The two seemed to be alone on a distant planet.

For a moment, Ashley and Josh locked on each other's eyes. The only sound was their light breathing, though Josh could have sworn that Ashley could have heard his heart beating. Facing each other, their hands lighting on the other's arms. Ashley caught a playful spark in Josh's eye, a childlike glimmer she had not seen since they met. For a moment, both of their lips quivered, parting slightly as if to speak, but no sounds made their way out.

Finally, Josh found his voice, almost disappointed to shatter the moment. "This is wonderful, thank you," he whispered.

Ashley opened her mouth to speak, but then closed, feeling her words undervalued the moment. Instead, she offered a warm smile in return. Standing still for the first time since they had arrived, a chill caught her. Seeing her shiver, Josh rubbed her arms vigorously. Her smiled turned sideways, Ashley smirked, "Thanks, that's one way to warm me up."

Abruptly, she whipped away, darting out from under the waterfall. Josh poked his head to see what she was up to. As he peered around the edge, he was promptly greeted with a wet, cold projectile against his chest. Looking down at his snow spattered jacket and then up at his attacker who wore an enormous grin, he wheeled back under the waterfall and swooped out the other side. Making a beeline for the bank, he scooped up a handful of snow. Before he could complete his armament, another ball came rocketing across the pond, smacking him in the thigh.

Locating on the giggling that followed the last volley, he spun he fired his own. Landing on Ashley's shoulder, the ball burst into a shower of snowy shrapnel that peppered the side of her head. Josh grimaced at the placement of his shot, stammering to apologize; he took a step in her direction. Looking up at him with a hurt expression on her face, Ashley suddenly gave a wicked grin as she pushed off on the ice in Josh's direction. To his surprise, Ashley leaped at him, tackling him onto the frozen surface, both of them spinning wildly on the ice.

Laughing hysterically, the pair lay on the ice, Ashley on top of Josh. "Isn't this how we met?" Josh grinned.

"Oh, that's it!" Ashley shrieked, plucking snow off her jacket and slipping it under Josh's collar.

Josh wriggled under his attacker, trying to get free to pull the snow out of his shirt. For a moment, their eyes locked again, each of them freezing. Josh could feel Ashley's warm breath on his lips. He could feel his pulse quicken as his gaze plunged into her deep blue eyes. Two impulses fought their way to his muscles. One was to push his head forward and press his lips against hers. The other, born from the pain of divorce and the years that followed –distancing from any relationship other than Kaya, won.

Sliding backward on the ice, he slipped out from under Ashley. Grasping her hands, he pulled her up to her knees and then stood them both up. The quiet in the blanket of snow was deafening as they stopped to catch their breath. Both tried to interpret the other's intentions, neither confident in their assessment. Josh wrapped his arm around Ashley's waist and with subtle pressure guided her toward the trailhead, "It's going to get dark quickly, we should probably head back."

"You're probably right," Ashley replied softly.

"This was an amazing afternoon, Ashley," Josh said and then noticing that the mood had sobered and Ashley's affect had eroded, snaked his hand out at an overhanging limb. The fir bough snapped in the air like a diving board, showering its cache of snow on Ashley's head. A playful scowl returned to her face as Josh shrugged with a sheepish grin, "I owed you."

As the SUV pulled into the parking lot of the Piccolo Paradiso coffee shop, conflict again rose within Josh. The day had been a magical surprise. He was thankful that he agreed to go with Ashley to Punchbowl Falls. The spot seemed even more magical than he had remembered, then again, this was also the only time he had gone with the infectious spirit and joy of Ashley. Putting the car in park, he felt his stomach twist into a knot. The same pulse-quickening highjack, his nervous system demanding he decide between fight or flight, that deadened the mood temporarily on the ice had returned. He was saved from committing to either.

Reaching across the console, Ashley spread her arms to hug Josh. "I had a really good time. Thanks for indulging me."

"Thank you. It was a great afternoon."

Ashley peeled away from the brief embrace, her face twisted in a quizzical expression, "I hope this isn't too forward, but tomorrow night is Hometown Holidays, I'm going to step away from the shop for a while to watch my niece. She and her class are singing elves in the downtown…anyway, I was wondering if you would want to come?"

"I uh…tomorrow night?" Josh stammered, somewhere in the dark recesses of his head called fight or flight? Fight or flight? "It sounds great. Thank you so much for inviting me…"

"But…" Ashley interjected, her voice trailing expectantly.

"I've got this family thing. I already blew them off today," Josh struggled with his words and then brightened, "Which, I am very glad I did."

Ashley smiled, "Family is important. Thanks for playing hooky with me today. Maybe we'll see each other again before you leave?"

"I'd like that, unless you're throwing another latte at me."

"Or shoving snow down your shirt?"

"You know, I didn't mind that part so much," Josh chuckled thoughtfully, "Enjoy your family tomorrow night."

"You too."

Josh watched as Ashley turned and opened the door. For a moment, like when she was at center ice at the pond, time seemed to stop. The light coming in from the streetlamp gave a sparkle to Ashley's blue eyes, made the faint freckles on the bridge of her nose shimmered, enhancing the warmth of her smile. The door closed, and time once more continued. When Ashley had reached her own car and slid into the driver's seat, Josh gave a quick wave and put the SUV in reverse.

The drive back to his parent's house was a blur. Josh's mind was clouded as he navigated the roadways. Snapping to attention, a blaze of taillights lit up the highway. Slowing the SUV, Josh could see that the traffic wound to the edge of the horizon. Taking advantage of being beside an exit, Josh flipped his turn signal and gunned the vehicle down the ramp. Twisting his way through the side streets, he worked his way past the traffic jam.

Squeezing the brakes, Josh directed the car to a stop at a red light, lights in the adjacent lawn caught his attention. A makeshift stable was lit to display two figures kneeling along either side of a crib. The posture and expressions of the figures captured the adoring love new parents have for their child. Outside of the stable, three more characters awaited their turn to gaze upon the newborn, each patiently holding out a gift. At the peak of the stable was a star. It was that lone star that housed the lighting for the set, bathing the scene in a soft glow.

Josh sighed as he thought about what he studied. All these years, he had pushed away the gifts, the music, decorations, the parties - all that the holidays brought. Here, on the side of the road was a part of Christmas that he realized was unfair to ignore. The love for this child that the artist had so well articulated in the figures on the lawn, reminded Josh of the Corinthians verse he cherished most, "Love is patient, love is kind. It always protects, always trusts, always hopes, always perseveres. Love never fails." Love never fails, yet he felt it had failed him. It failed Kaya and the cohesive family life she deserved. Somehow, staring at the nativity, Josh felt his bitterness might have been misguided.

The light turned to green, and Josh returned his attention to the road. Pulling away from the stop, Josh thought of what Christmas at the core was really about. He told himself that he needed to find a way to honor that part of the holidays, especially when he was with Kaya and his family.

"Hi, Daddy!" Kaya's voice squealed into the phone.

"How was your day, sweetheart? Tell me about it."

"Well, Roger made waffles this morning. They were pretty good…I'd rather have your Macadamia nut pancakes, though. Then we played in the snow. Mom helped me make a snowman while Roger shoveled the driveway. After that, we just hung out in the house, making cookies and stuff. Mom said I could make a box of them for you. I think you'll like them," Kaya declared.

"I'm sure I will. I can't wait."

"What did you do today? I missed you," Kaya blurted.

"I missed you too, honey," Josh sighed, and thought about the day, "Well, I went to spend some time at a coffee shop. I met a friend there who reminded me about a place that I used to go around here as a kid."

"A friend? Who?"

"Her name is Ashley. I kind of met her yesterday when she spilled coffee on me."

"That's a funny way to meet somebody."

"Yes, I guess it is," Josh chuckled, "So Ashley suggested we drive out to Punch Bowl Falls. It is all frozen right now and is really spectacular. The entire forest is painted white. The pond was frozen solid – enough that we could walk out on it. The best was the waterfall; it was completely frozen in place, so much that you could walk all the way behind it."

"Wow, that sounds really neat. I want to see it," Kaya grinned through the phone.

"I'd love to take you some time; I think you would like it."

"Ashley sounds fun," Kaya stated abruptly.

"She is. She even started a snowball fight. I think you would like her," Josh admitted.

"You sound happy, Daddy," Kaya affirmed, "Goodnight. Call me tomorrow."

"Goodnight, sweetheart," Josh's words trailed off as his impetuous daughter had already clicked the phone off.

Her words hung in his mind. Their conversation, so simple on the surface, resounded in him. The frankness of Kaya's assessment of his mood, the perceptiveness that his daughter had simply by listening to him over the phone, seemed more astute and clear than his own thoughts. As he leaned against the windowsill, tracing the moonlight on the snow-covered lawn, he thought, maybe Kaya was.

Chapter Seven

The scent of coffee wafted into the den, providing Josh a pleasant awakening. Sitting up, he heard the clanging of pans in the kitchen. A glance at his watch that laid on the desk confirmed that this was the latest he had slept the entire time he had been there. With a long stretch and yawn, he thought to himself that it was the best he had slept too.

Pulling on pajama bottoms and a T-shirt, he shuffled towards the kitchen. Leaning in, he kissed his mother as she flipped a pancake over on the skillet.

"Good morning, sleepyhead!" his mother crooned, "I was about to send Noah and Sarah in to wake you."

"Good morning Uncle Josh!" the kids chorused, "It's Christmas tree day!"

"It is?" Josh exclaimed, rubbing each on their already tussled heads, then pausing as it dawned on him what they had said, "Hey, don't we already have a tree?"

"Grandpa and Grandma have a tree. We are going to get one for Mrs. Wilson," Noah announced.

"The neighbor across the street," Amy filled her brother in, "Mr. Wilson passed this year, and she doesn't have any way to get one."

"It's a surprise!" Noah added triumphantly.

"We're gonna pick the biggest, prettiest tree we can find!" Sarah proudly added.

"Uncle Josh used to team up with Grandpa on tree picking. I think they were on the constant search for the Charlie Brown tree," Amy chided.

"I remember that movie. That was a tiny tree!" exclaimed Noah.

"Yes, but then it turned beautiful!" Sarah added triumphantly.

"I liked our trees," Josh defended, his voice distant in his coffee mug.

Nicholas stomped into the kitchen from the garage, his untied work boots thumping with every step on the floor. He looked a bit silly, clad with a heavy jacket, gloves, and hand saw. "I liked our trees too! Amy and your Mom just wanted trees that were so big we had to lop the top off to the point they were no longer Christmas trees, more like fat, stubby Christmas shrubs."

Josh shot a proud look past the children at their mother, who shrugged.

"I'm glad you are coming, Uncle Josh," Noah gushed.

"Hey," Sarah suddenly sported a quizzical look across her jelly speckled face, "Where were you yesterday, Uncle Josh?"

"Yeah, we missed you," Noah nodded his head vigorously.

"I was…visiting a place I hadn't been in years," Josh narrated, "Have you guys ever been to Punch Bowl Falls? It is a beautiful place in the mountains with this huge waterfall that ends up in this near perfectly round pool, kind of like a bowl. It's neat in the summertime when the water is rushing in, in the winter, it takes on an even more magical transformation – the entire waterfall is frozen solid as is the pool that it empties into. There is snow all around it; it's kind of like being in your very own snow globe."

"Wow, it sounds great!" Sarah shrieked.

"Yeah, will you take us?" Noah chimed.

"If it works into our Christmas schedule, I know there is still lots to do before Santa comes," Josh declared.

As the kids nodded, Josh felt as though he had escaped further questioning. Then Sarah cocked her head in his direction, "Uncle Josh, did you go there by yourself?"

"Yeah, Uncle Josh, did you go there by yourself?" Amy echoed, an eyebrow raised and a crooked smile crossing her face.

"Well, no. A friend I met at a coffee shop went with me," Josh answered, suddenly feeling himself in a repeat conversation to the one he had with Kaya the night before.

"Who?" Sarah quizzed.

"She works there. I think she felt bad about spilling coffee on me the last time I was there."

"Oh. Why'd she spill coffee on you?" Sarah continued her interrogation.

"It was an accident. Now I think the two of you need to finish your breakfast so that we can go find Mrs. Wilson a magical tree," Josh said firmly to ward off further inquiry and shooting a glance to his sister, "That goes for you too."

"What? We're just curious where you disappear to. We love you, Uncle Josh," Amy grinned.

"Yeah, we love you, Uncle Josh!" the kids chorused.

"Alright, alright. Eat your breakfast. I'm going to go shower," Josh stated as he filled his coffee mug and headed down the hall.

Carol pulled her gloves on and grabbed her purse, "Ready to go? Knowing our family, this could be quite the journey."

Inside his own head, Josh rolled his eyes and sighed heavily. He prepared for another day immersed in Christmas cheer with his family. Given his current holiday disposition, he couldn't think of a harsher sentence. At least he'd have fun with the kids Josh reluctantly resigned.

The Christmas tree farm overflowed with families toting sleds packed with either kids, saws, or in one case, a smiling family dog. Sarah and Noah burst out of the SUV and were already scanning the trees from the parking lot.

Joshed helped Nick unload the sled and offered the pull the children as they piled inside it. Bob seemed especially pleased to have his brother-in-law along for the occasion. Amy was already pulling her mother towards the map, which showed the varieties planted.

"What do you think, a thirty-footer should do under Mrs. Wilson's eight-foot living room ceiling…" Josh teased.

"Hmmm, that would be the Daniels' tradition, wouldn't it? There has to be something completely wacky about it," Amy laughed.

"Let the kids pick. I have a hunch they would be far more adept," Josh reasoned.

Amy mocked a look of amazement, "Wow, little brother, you have become sage in your old age. Impressive."

Biting his lip on a reply, he instead wrapped his fist in a single blow against the wooden map, causing the little cornice that had built along its top edge to cascade down on top of his sister. Sarah and Noah burst into laughter as their mom shrieked under the shower of snow.

"I retract that last comment," Amy pouted, "But having the kids pick is still a pretty prudent idea."

Bob patted Josh on the shoulder, offering an approving grin. The gesture met with Amy rifling a snowball into her husband's shoulder. Bob was aghast, "He did it!"

"You married her, sorry pal," Josh dismissed the protest.

Amy shot Josh an evil look, causing her brother to put his hands up in defense, "Not sorry he married you, sis. Just in that it comes with its price."

"Well worth it, surely," Nick entered the conversation.

"Humph!" Amy crossed her arms in defiance, "If you weren't pulling the sled and hauling the tree, why…I'd have no use for you three today!"

"I thought it was funny, Uncle Josh," Sarah beamed from the sled.

Amy cast her daughter a disgusted glare, mumbling, "Traitor!"

Josh's wisdom was accurate as the adults led the family to trees that warped on one side, had brown needles, or didn't have a prayer of fitting in the house. Noah and Sarah ran a few quiet laps around the Douglas Firs before arriving at one at the same time. "This one!" They giggled.

The family gathered around, each admiring the children's choice. "It's perfect," Carol said.

Nick and Bob looked at each other and then handed Josh the saw. "My back," Nick shrugged, "And Bob…"

Josh waved his arms and accepted the saw, "I got it."

Sliding under the tree, Josh settled on the snow and began working the saw through the stump of the tree. In moments, he had the saw nearly clean through the tree. He climbed out from under the tree and stood beside his niece and nephew, each wearing a puzzled look.

"Uhh, Uncle Josh, it's still connected to the ground," Sarah tapped at his sleeve.

Josh looked startled and shot the tree a confused glance. "Oh," he grinned at the kids, "I almost forgot the final step."

Taking a small step backward, he planted his foot and launched himself at the tree in a giant tackle, sending it himself to the ground in a triumphant crash. The kids erupted in a chorus of cheers and giggles. "There," Josh smiled as he dusted himself off.

Amy shook her head, "You're a nut, little brother."

"I think you made a nice choice, guys," Josh patted his niece and nephew on their shoulders.

Hoisting the tree off the ground, Josh and plopped it on the sled. The kids looked puzzled. They hadn't considered they would lose their ride to the tree. Josh noticed their perplexity and swooped in with a solution. Snatching each up in the air, he swung them on top of the tree as though they were riding on some giant green toboggan.

As he tugged the laden sled back to the entrance, Josh's mind wandered. He had to admit to himself that he enjoyed his family today. Focusing on his niece and nephew was a bittersweet resolve. He wished he were able to share these experiences with Kaya. In his heart, he knew that is how it should be, and any other scenario was just nonsensical.

He had caught his mind occasionally wandering – as though he had somewhere else to be. He assumed he had just been thinking of Kaya, but there was something else. Someone else. He shook his head, dismissing that thought. He didn't have room in his life for that. Not right now. Yet somehow, Ashley found a way to make appearances in his mind - the image of her grinning against the backdrop of the waterfall. Josh could swear her perfume still hung in the air. He could feel her breath against his. Almost angry with himself, he shook her pictures from his mind.

Her brother's head shake caught Amy's attention. "Talking to yourself there, Joshy?"

"What…oh, uh, no?" Josh winced.

"I saw you shaking your head. Like you could ever get your mind off something once you caught the scent," Amy pried, "What is it?"

"Nothing. Just wishing Kaya was here," Josh answered.

Amy slung her arm around her brother's shoulder, "I know. I'm glad you're here, anyway. Sarah and Noah sure have enjoyed you being around."

"It has been nice to spend time with them," Josh admitted, "All of you."

The last words producing a warm smile across Amy's face, she leaned into her brother and gave him a tight hug.

Despite Josh's resistance, delivering the tree to Mrs. Wilson was a special treat. When the widow opened the door and saw the Daniels' family standing in her doorway, the widow burst into tears. Welcoming them in, she disappeared down the hall, leaving the Daniels standing in the foyer, passing confused looks to each other as to what they should do.

The sound of dishware clattering in the kitchen concluded with the clang of a kettle on the stove. Mrs. Wilson hustled back in the room to rejoin her guests. “I put some water on for tea and cocoa,” she announced.

“Mrs. Wilson, you didn’t have to do that,” Carol protested.

“Nonsense, it’s the least I can do. I can’t believe you brought me a tree. This year without…without…”

Carol put her arms around her neighbor and hugged her, “I know.”

“It was really the kids’ idea. They always commented on how beautiful your tree looked each year in your front window. We hope you don’t mind…,” Carol admitted.

“I’m touched, really,” Mrs. Wilson said, sitting down on her sofa as the emotions settled.

“If you like, we could help you decorate,” Sarah said softly.

“You know, dear, I would love that.”

“My, Josh. I am glad you made it home this year. I think a little piece of your mother’s heart has been broken each year without you,” Mrs. Wilson said, holding her hand for Josh to grasp, “How is that sweet daughter of yours?”

“She is…amazing, Mrs. Wilson. She spends the holiday with her mother,” Josh shrugged.

“So you’re a little heartbroken each Christmas too,” the widow presumed.

Josh paused, looking into the kind woman’s face and admitted, “Yes, ma’am, more than a little.”

"You have turned into a fine young man, not that little imp that used to knock over our trash cans playing football in the street. No, Carol tells me you are a terrific father."

"Thank you. The credit goes to Kaya. She makes being a dad easy – and wonderful," Josh said, "Mrs. Wilson, can I get the decorations for you?"

"That would be wonderful. They are tucked away in the garage by the furnace. There is a tree stand there as well," and then as if some sudden inspiration swept over her, she pushed herself out of her seat, "I have no idea how buried those things might be, I better help you find your way."

"I can manage," Josh assured her, but the woman persisted. With Carol offering to pour the tea and coffee, Mrs. Wilson and Josh made their way through the garage, squeezing past and old Chrysler that appeared as though it hadn't moved in years.

The elderly woman pointed at a stack of boxes neatly marked as Christmas items. On top of them sat the stand as she had predicted.

"It was hard for me, holidays without Harold," Mrs. Wilson declared. Josh was struck by the abrupt nature of the sentiment, but quietly allowed her to continue. "I didn't want them to come. Whether it was the Fourth of July, Thanksgiving or heaven forbid, our anniversary. I didn't want those days without Harold. But along the way, I realized that wishing them away wasn't unfair only to myself, but to those who cared for me, never mind Harold himself. He would be ashamed at how I handled myself wallowing away without him. He would be sad. I don't know how I came to realize that, but once I did, I began to feel his warmth on those days; I began to celebrate them once again. Not in spite of him, but for him."

"He would surely not be ashamed of you now, Mrs. Wilson," Josh assured.

"I should think not," Mrs. Wilson beamed, and then her face fell to concern, "I see the pain in you. Obviously, in a different way, but I know that ache. I know that avoidance."

"When Kaya was a baby, I could almost envision our Christmases almost as though I was flipping through a photo album," Josh admitted softly, "It just isn't supposed to be this way."

"Of course, it isn't. But a secret?" Mrs. Wilson reduced her voice to a whisper, "Nothing ever is."

Mrs. Wilson's keen words stuck in Josh's mind most of the day. When they had finished helping her with the tree and cleaned up the cocoa and tea, Josh thanked her and wished her a Merry Christmas. Retreating across the street to his parents' house, Josh grabbed his phone out of his pocket as it buzzed.

At first, he didn't recognize the number. He knew the area code was the same as his folks,' but it wasn't Dana's number.

Josh read the text, "Just in case you change your mind, the invitation is still out there. Merry Christmas, Ashley."

Josh paused momentarily, his thumb circling the reply button on the phone, hovering over it several times only to close it and place it back in his pocket.

"Who was that, Josh? Someone in Hawaii?" Amy pried, and then her eyes widened, "The mystery coffee woman?"

At first, it seemed as though Josh was ignoring his sister, but then almost absently replied, "No one." His mind wandered for just a moment, mulling over the possibility of seeing Ashley again. His sister's comments only caused the discomfort Josh felt about seeing a woman again to ferment stronger.

Josh tried to engross himself in his family's environment – playing with the children, helping his Mom and Amy in the kitchen, or burying himself in a random magazine that was lying around – he just couldn't shake his distracted melancholy.

He found himself checking his phone, but for what? His text box still has Ashley's message on top. I almost felt guilty for not responding. She seemed like a nice woman, very attractive, yet he couldn't bring himself to open that door any further. Besides, with her on the mainland and he in Hawaii, a brief interlude it would be at best. And that did not interest him in the least.

His restlessness finally getting the best of him, he borrowed his father's car again to wander the town. Parking at the edge of the downtown marketplace, he aimlessly followed the crowd that had begun to gather for the Hometown Holidays festivities. Walking past the historic Liberty Theater and antique shops, he would occasionally stick his head into one, sorting through the memorabilia. He tried to hunt for presents for his family, but he found himself continually finding things for Kaya instead, leaving him even less inspired and lonelier.

Between shops, the chill from the wind would snake its way through any and every gap in his clothing, forcing him to shiver in response. Almost subconsciously, he found himself outside of the coffee shop. Planting himself on the sidewalk, Josh anguished about his next move.

Inside, he could see Ashley interacting with her customers. He smile radiant and genuine, sharing it with everyone she spoke to her. He watched as the patrons reacted to her, even those who appeared weary from a day's work or shopping seemed to trade their tetchy visages for smiles of their own. Energy seemed to well back within them. Josh couldn't help but be all over again impressed.

Josh was almost lost in his accidental voyeurism until Ashley grabbed her coat and began making her way towards the door. A glance at his watch told Josh that she was heading out for her niece's Christmas play.

In a moment of panic, Josh's brain reeled, fight or flight once more kicking him in the head, spurring action one way or the other. One hand reaching for the door handle, one foot aiming to propel him away, flashes of greeting her, and disappearing into the evening competed for results. Ashley's gregarious nature bought Josh valuable time, as she paused to speak with several of her guests on the way towards the door.

One impulse finally taking hold, Josh pulled the collar up on his jacket and allowed himself to melt away into the crowd. His hands clammy, sweat beading on his brow; Josh walked on, destination unknown. Away.

Camas' little downtown area had become awash in families and couples. Stores offered chocolates, candy canes, and cocoa to the visitors. The town's dignitaries stationed in front of the theater, where a towering evergreen waited to be lit for the evening. Each block had a section where school children would sing, or bands would play Christmas songs. Children streamed out of the downtown church with ornaments volunteers helped them make. If not for sheer panic to escape unseen, Josh might have enjoyed the scene. Then again, without Kaya, the family revelry may only have served to plummet his mood further.

Slipping down a side street, Josh made his way out of the crowds and back to his father's car. Turning the ignition, he fled the market. Josh mindlessly followed traffic, merging onto the highway, he almost felt as though he were driving toward comfort. A growing feeling of excitement, a sense of impending contentment fingered through his veins, almost forcing a smile in spite of himself. Then as he saw the exit sign, he realized why. He was driving towards Dana's house. For a few moments, he allowed the car to continue that course. Just one look, one peek to see Kaya. See her perfect smiling face. See that she was okay.

"No." The word echoed through his head. He knew it was wrong. He just missed her so much. For a moment, he could almost remember what the Christmas season was like with his daughter. Her excitement, drinking in every decoration, and singing with all of her heart to every Christmas carol. Snuggling on the couch with her cocoa as they admired their tree, her eyes twinkling in the strung lights.

These happiest of thoughts made his heart sink lower than ever. Finding a break in the traffic, Josh spun the car around and re-entered the highway.

Once more, giving in to the flow of traffic, he stopped just outside of downtown. Drawn, as he so often was when contemplating something, he found himself at the riverfront park. Walking along the snow-swept path, tracked the curving river which had crusted over with ice. A few inches below, he could still hear the water flowing underneath.

The park along the narrow canal was stunning. The trees were all flocked with snow, as was the river, coating the ice. A soft flurry of snow drifted downward, a target for children with tongues protruded as far out as they could stretch.

Emotionally exhausted, mentally frustrated, Josh plopped onto a bench facing the water. Leaning back against the seat, he allowed the winter scene to steal his mind. Peace slowly infiltrated, thoughts consumed by images. Nature staking its claim in Josh's head, he drifted into a pleasant numbness. For a while, as brief as it were, Josh was in a peaceful winterland. His soul calm, as it was, it was in season's past.

Night had settled in around him. For some time, Josh had been largely unaware of those he shared the park. As most workdays had come to an end, families began populating then trail more. Local residents used the beautiful channel as their path to shops and restaurants.

Josh watched as dads held their daughters' hands or gave their son's piggybacks. Wives would huddle close, snaking their arms into their husbands, escaping the chilling breeze. Couples giggled as they made their holiday plans or teased about the secret surprises they had already stashed under their trees.

The sights and sounds that had smashed his brief solace and serenity were bittersweet. Josh did not resent any for having their families, their loved ones with them. Yet, he felt only more hollow in himself for what he now lacked. All at once, he was desperate to be back in Hawaii. Losing himself in the pounding waves, exhausting himself in the relentless tide.

His phone beeped, momentarily, he thought of Ashley. Shaking the thought off, he felt she had surely replaced him one of any number of suitors by now. He hoped she had. He hoped she was having a good time watching her niece.

Sliding his phone free of its pocket, he saw that it was Dana's. She sent a text saying that Kaya wanted to say hi.

Smiling as broad as he had all day, he pressed the call back button. "Daddy!" a little voice squealed into the phone.

"Hi, sweetheart."

"I know it's not bedtime, but I wanted to talk to you. I miss you, Daddy," Kaya called into the phone.

"I miss you too, Kaya," Josh replied.

"Did you have a good day? Mom and Roger took me on the Polar Express train ride. It was pretty cool. You would have liked it. I know you think the characters in the movie are a little creepy, and they are, the ones on the train weren't at all," Kaya shared excitedly into the phone.

"That's good."

"Yeah, anyway, we had fun, but I missed you. I wish you could have come too!"

"That would have been fun. I'm glad you had such a good time," Josh agreed.

"What about you? What did you do? How are Sara and Noah?"

"They are good. They helped get a tree for Mrs. Wilson across the street from Grandpa and Grandmas."

"I like Mrs. Wilson. She always has funny stories about you when you were a kid!"

"Yes. Yes, she does. She likes you too, by the way, Josh replied.

"That was nice of you to get a tree for her. Very Christmassy, Daddy!" Kaya exclaimed.

Josh couldn't help but laugh at his daughter's zeal and keen insight into her father's psyche. "I let you put lights around one of our palm trees at home."

"Yeah, but we use it for the Fourth of July and everything else too!"

"Hmm, bah humbug Cindy Lou Who!" Josh teased.

"Funny daddy. I know you love Christmas. I just think you lost it when Mommy left."

"When you leave," Josh whispered.

"What daddy?"

"Nothing."

"Did you see…uh…Ashley?" Kaya asked.

"No. I just…"

"Why not? She sounded nice!" Kaya demanded.

"Well, she, uh…I…" Josh stammered, "I was busy!"

"What are you doing now?"

"Sitting in a park."

"By yourself?"

"Well, there are other people here…"

"You know, Daddy, I miss you too at Christmas. That's why I had Mom call you," Kaya shared and then added, her tone directive, "You should have some fun!"

"I am fine, Kaya," Josh declared sternly, and then softened, "I love you, sweetheart."

"I love you too, Daddy," Kaya spoke her words, soft and sweet, "I should probably go now, Mom and Roger are setting up a game. I'll talk to you tomorrow."

The phone fell silent. Josh tucked it away in his pocket. He let in a sigh, not as shuddering and cold as they had been. He suddenly felt the weight he had unwittingly placed on his daughter's shoulders was a tax too heavy for such a young, sweet child. He never wanted her to see how much he hurt, but he knew she was too perceptive, or he had moped a bit too much. Almost more provoking, was how sound her words were. She was an incredibly bright, genuinely caring young woman. He was blessed to have a daughter like Kaya. That thought was nothing new to him, but one that fueled him since her arrival eight of years ago. A thought that often carried him through some days.

Chapter Eight

Sarah set her juice drink down and looked at her uncle with a glance. "Are you gonna come with us to see Santa and his reindeer?"

"There is a farm near here that helps Santa get a few of his reindeer in Christmas Eve shape. We're going to go check them out. They have sleigh rides for the kids, cider and all kinds of fun things," Amy explained.

Carol looked up from the dish she was drying, curious to her son's response.

"Yeah, I'd love to go," Josh agreed, sliding in a chair next to the kids. Both Sarah and inching closer to their uncle.

His immediate approval of the event caught Amy and Carol by surprise. Carol smiled quietly as she resumed wiping the dish she was holding.

The farm bustled with families eager to spend time with Santa's reindeer before their busy night. The entire Daniels clan made their way to the stable where the animals appeared to Josh as quite ordinary creatures. Smaller than he anticipated, each more or less oblivious to the crowd who watched them as they mindlessly chewed on hay that covered nearly every inch of the stable.

"They won't talk because we're here," Sarah explained from her perch atop Josh's shoulders.

"Oh," her brother nodded, sitting similarly atop his father.

"Well, yeah. I mean, have you ever seen an elf?"Josh asked, "No, because they all have to do their work without us knowing it's them. That kind of spoils magic."

"I'm a little scared of elves. They are always watching us," Noah declared.

"Well, you only have to be afraid of them if you're not behaving. Your mom should have been petrified of them when we were kids!" Josh explained, promptly receiving a retaliatory swat on the arm from his sister.

"See?" he grinned.

"Were you, Mom?" Noah asked.

"Nah, I was an angel. Your Uncle Josh, on the other hand…let's just say I always got more toys than him," Amy replied, giving Josh and a squinty smile.

"Neither of you two are getting presents this year if you don't straighten up!" Carol interceded.

"Who do you suppose they are?" Nicholas asked as he squeezed between his grandkids. Sarah and Noah took turns naming the half dozen reindeer, explaining why they thought they had identified the proper reindeer with the correct name.

Relinquishing their spots to the growing crowd behind them, the Daniels headed out of the stable. Following signs of playful plywood elves pointing in the direction of the various activities, they made their way to the skating pond, stopping for hot cocoas along the way.

The kids and the ladies quickly donned skates while the men decided they had better watch from the safety of a bench alongside the pond. Their respite did not last long as the pleas of Noah and Sarah were too much, drawing them off their perch. Begrudgingly, Bob and Nicholas found skates approximately their size and wobbled their way onto the ice. Josh hesitated, watching fathers help their children get into their skates as families prepared to play. Without Kaya, Josh just felt silly. He wanted to play with his niece and nephew, but he reasoned this was Bob and Amy's time with their kids. Recusing himself, he volunteered to take pictures as the rest of the clan took to the ice. Josh was rewarded by watching his father and brother-in-law spend more time on their hind ends than on their feet.

Before long, the adults were exhausted, Carol agreeing to remain in skates to help her grandbabies. As Bob and Nicholas returned their skates, Amy plopped down next to her bother. "You alright? You seem a little distracted."

"Do I?" Josh questioned, not feeling as though he had been.

"Sarah and Noah unable to coax you onto the ice, a little distant for much of the day," Amy added, "Just making sure you're okay."

Shrugging, Josh admitted, "I think so. I don't know, I'm fine."

"Alright, little brother. I'm here if you need to talk." She looked at Josh hard, as if trying to see inside him.

Josh sat silently beside his sister. Watching the kids circle the pond, while his mother spiraled in place trying to keep an eye on them. Amy's observation of him started to rattle in his head. He felt okay. In fact, he felt better about being home than he had the entire trip. Almost content, yet there was something gently tugging from the back of his mind.

When the kids had finally tired and their grandmother thoroughly dizzy from following their laps around the ice, the family reconvened. Amy suggested that it would be a good movie night. Bob scrolled through his phone, reading off the kids movies that were in the theaters. As one piqued Sarah and Noah's interests, they polled the family. As the consensus built, they turned to Josh.

"Josh?" Bob asked, not receiving a response repeated himself to his mentally distant brother-in-law, "Josh?"

"What? Oh – the movie... You know, I will let you guys go to the movie. I think I have somewhere to be," Josh replied, seeming to convince himself of that at that very moment.

"You do? More Christmas shopping?" his mother asked.

Amy cast a suspicious look at her brother. Her gut decided to bail him out, somehow thinking that whatever he had on his mind was necessary for him. "Actually, I sent him on a mission while you were still on the ice. We'll let my elf do what he needs tonight. We'll see you later, right?"

Josh flashed his sister a quick smile, "Yes. You guys have fun," kneeling to the kids, "I want a full report of the movie when I get back!"

"Without his long legs in the backseat, we can all fit in our SUV," Bob offered. Josh's father dug out his keys and tossed them in his son's direction.

Keys in hand, Josh set off for the parking lot. Unconsciously, he walked with a purpose. Glancing at his watch, he knew that Ashley prepared the shop for closing. Slipping behind the wheel, he made his way toward the coffee shop. The evening traffic was thick as Josh reached town, having to slow as people made their way home from work or to the mall for last-minute Christmas shopping. The taillights made him anxious as he continued studying his watch.

Peeling down a side road, he snaked his ways towards the coffee shop. Finally, wheeling the car into a parking space, he hopped out and burst through the door. Waiting behind the line, Josh peered above the small crowd hoping to catch a glance of Ashley. Behind the bar was a girl he had not seen before. Hearing a male voice at the register, he knew that Ashley wasn't there either. Dejected, he was afraid that he had missed her and the opportunity to accept the offer to join her and her family at the carnival.

As the line thinned, a voice called out, "Josh, right?" Josh looked up to see Ashley's co-worker Dan.

"Yeah, you're Dan?" he acknowledged, "Is Ashley here?"

"Aw man, you just missed her. Maybe...ten, maybe fifteen minutes ago?"

"I was afraid of that," Josh said in a sullen voice. Ordering a coffee, he wondered if he should catch up with his family. Being at the coffee shop had given him such a warm feeling. He realized, though, that this feeling was different from the familiar solace that he had sought and found on his first visit. This one was different. This one filled him with anxious anticipation – butterflies that tried to suppress even from himself.

As he walked toward the door, he paused. Turning, he caught Dan's eye, "Would you know which school Ashley's nephew goes to?"

"Sure, up at Crown Park – it's right up the hill before you get to the lake."

Josh thanked him and pushed his way through the door. Jumping back in his father's vehicle, he spun the tires as they fought for traction on the slick surface. He felt his pulse quicken as he committed to his decision. The butterflies, whose existence he tried to deny, intensified into a flock wild birds.

As he neared the park, the excitement of joining Ashley was suddenly intermingled with doubt whether he should interrupt her family outing. For all he knew, she might have invited someone else in his place, or simply the dynamic of him just showing up might not be welcomed by her and her family. Passing a line of cars parked along the street, Josh was half looking for a parking space and half looking for a place to turn around. As if a sign telling him just to shut up and park, a car pulled from the curb right in front of him. Turning the wheel, he slid the car into the vacated space.

Joining a crowded event solo, never mind to find a woman he had turned down to attend the event, was very foreign to Josh. The warm bubbly nature of Ashley spurred him along in his head. Her spirit was infectious, and Josh enjoyed being with her, enough to brave a crowd of families getting into the Christmas festivities.

Josh walked up to the entrance and paid his donation to the school PTA. Once inside the grounds, he was amazed at the festive scene that sprawled the expanse of the park. Josh was impressed, for a school run event, it was a massive undertaking. In one area, nearly twenty snowmen stood lining the main walkway, maintain vigil for an apparent judging. A snow hill fitted with a tow rope was jammed with a procession of anxious children waiting to make the ride, each hugging a massive inner tube. Dozens of vendors sold handmade gifts and holiday treats. Somewhere in the carnival, Josh could hear a Santa Clause bellowing his hearty ho-ho-hos. In the very center of the park, a four-inch pool had been framed, filled and frozen into a sizable skating rink, two giant ice sculpture reindeer marked either side of the entrance. Next to one of the reindeer, Josh spotted Ashley.

As he took a few steps forward, he watched her interacting with her friends and family. Suddenly a wave of hesitation consumed him, suddenly feeling uninvited and out of place. He paused, unsure of whether he should interrupt her time with her family. Shaking his head, he turned to take his first step away.

"Josh?" a voice called out from behind him.

Josh stopped in his tracks and wheeled around sheepishly, "I…I didn't want to interrupt."

"I didn't expect to see you," Ashley beamed.

Looking flustered, Josh' cheeks reddened. Asking meekly, "Is the invitation still open?"

"Yes, of course, it is!" Ashley offered with a big smile. Striding away from the group, she held out her hands to grasp his, "I'm glad you came." Tugging his hands gently, she led him toward the group she had been standing near.

Josh was flush with nerves, as he followed Ashley he noticed each one of the people she was with had stopped what they were doing and stood watching them. "So this is the guy you threw coffee at and then tackled?" a young woman asked, her obviously taking Josh in.

"Yeah, something like that," Ashley nodded.

"And he still wants to hang out with you? Must have bumped his head when he hit the floor," a tall, thin man joked.

"Guys, I would like you to meet Josh. And yes, he is the one I told you about," Ashley addressed the group sternly and then swept her outstretched hand in a circle at them, "Josh, this is my brother Andrew, his wife Lori and this cutie is Christa."

Josh exchanged hellos to everyone; Christa peered at him from behind the safety of her mother's waist. Andrew clapped his hand on Josh's shoulder, "Come on. We were just about to throw our hat in the ring for the snowman contest."

The lighthearted, yet demonstrative reception from Ashley's family stifled most of the nervousness that had held siege in Josh's stomach. A feeling of warmth instead began to take hold in him, a sense he was starting to get used to when he was near Ashley.

Falling in step with the family, Josh and Ashley lagged just behind. Snaking one arm through his, while affectionately pressing her other hand against his chest as they walked, Ashley looked up at Josh, "I can't believe you came."

"I could smell the apple cider donuts from town. To be honest, I forgot you said you were going to be here," Josh teased, slipping his hand against her back.

"Admit it, you kind of like me," Ashley's eyes lit up as she stood on her tiptoes to get closer to his eye level.

"You're alright, but apple cider donuts…"

"You are begging for another snowball fight!" Ashley laughed, "I hope you're good at snowman making. My family takes their holiday stuff pretty seriously."

"I better stick to the ball rolling. Let you guys handle the detail work."

Andrew stopped the procession in front of a six-foot square space among the growing army of snowmen Josh saw when he had arrived. As Andrew divvied out instructions, the family began taking their respective roles in the snowman making process. The task of making the family snowman brought everyone together, laughing, playing, joking…eradicating any feelings of awkwardness that Josh had felt entering the carnival.

He diligently worked on the two giant snowballs that would become the torso and midsection of their frosty creation while Andrew set on crafting the ideal top ball for the head. The girls were already lining out the accessories that were going to adorn their man when the boys had completed their part. As Josh heaved the middle ball on top of the larger bottom one, Ashley and Lori began packing snow in between to seal the two together.

Ready, Andrew placed his perfectly round ball on top. Standing back, he and Josh watched the ladies take over. His arms crossed, admiring the efforts taking place, "Ashley tells me you have a little girl."

Beaming proudly, Josh nodded, "Kaya, she's eight."

"Man, its great, isn't it? Having kids…they keep us young!" Andrew sighed.

"That they do," Josh agreed.

"Plus, it's nice having an excuse to act like a kid when you have one, right?" Andrew grinned. As the finishing touches were added to their snow person, Andrew walked up and slung an arm around his wife and daughter, admiring their handiwork.

Ashley slunk over to Josh, "Nice bottom."

Josh shot her a quizzical look and quickly received a smack on the shoulder and a scowl from Ashley, "The legs and body of our snowman."

"I know," Josh grinned and added, "Nice family."

"Thank you, I kind of like them. They're my best friends. I don't typically bring strange men around to meet them, you know," she whispered.

"Just sad sacks who avoid Christmas?" Josh asked.

"We'll see. You're here, aren't you," Ashley smiled as her brother's family took one last look at the snowman and congratulated each other on their efforts. Pleased with their endeavor, they left their creation for judging.

Christa, Ashley's niece, looked up at Josh, "Are you good at skating?"

"I used to be. I could probably still manage," Josh shrugged.

"Good, then you're with me," Christa declared and grabbed his hand. Ashley watched and smiled at the exchange as her niece towed Josh toward the skating rink.

With his toes crunched in hockey skates a size too small, Josh helped Christa onto the ice. "Are you a good skater?" he asked the six-year-old girl.

"Nope. You're going to have to stick with me." With a glance at Ashley, who had just finished lacing her skates, Christa held Josh's hand tight as the two began to circle the rink. As they completed their first lap, Ashley sped by them and spun around, skating backward.

"Having fun?" Ashley called, gracefully floating along the ice in front of them.

"Yes!" Christa snapped and curtly added, "I think Dad wants to skate with you, Aunt Ashley."

"Oh, you do, do you? I think your dad is just fine as I saw him skating with your mom right over there. Speaking of, I think you have had enough time with Josh on the ice. It is my turn," Ashley replied.

"But he's helping me," Christa said, her voice adopting a weak, pleading tone.

"Really? Who won the peewee figure skating contest the last two years in a row?"

"I don't know," Christa shrugged, looking up at Josh with a mischievous smile.

"You have been snowed, Josh. But don't feel bad, you aren't the first boy Christa has lured with her charm," Ashley smiled, spinning back to facing forward and grabbing his hand, "Come on, my turn."

"Hmmm, wonder where she gets that from," Josh asked as they glided forward. Ashley shrugged, her eyes dancing mischievously in the glow of the Christmas lights.

Hand in hand, they circled the rink, occasionally harassed by Christa, who would rocket by, spinning pirouettes as she passed. Josh felt like a kid again, holding hands with his date as he ice skated, yet somehow not at all uncomfortable being with Ashley and her family.

Ashley looked up at Josh, "Christa has a crush on you, you know."

"Jealous?"

"Absolutely," Ashley grinned, giving Josh a squeeze.

Taking enough laps to be thoroughly dizzy, Christa's parents urged her off of the ice. Hearing that the snowman judging was about to begin, the group hustled to the grandstand. As they waited for the winners to be announced, Christa edged her way in between Ashley and Josh prompting a giggle from her aunt. They cheered as the best in show, largest and most unusual prizes were read off. The emcee read off the winner of the best traditional snowman, the number for their plot rang through the loudspeaker. Christa shrieked and hugged Josh before hugging each of her parents and her aunt.

"Should we celebrate with donuts and hot apple cider?" Josh asked.

"After we take a picture with our snowman," Ashley's sister insisted, "You too stranger, you were part of our victory."

Begrudgingly, Josh complied and joined the group as a neighboring contestant fired a few shots from Lori's camera. After a series of photos, Josh offered to take a turn behind the camera, capturing the family just themselves.

As the pictures were done, donuts and cider were consumed; Christa's parents declared it was probably time that they head home. Ashley looked into Josh's eyes, "I don't suppose you'd mind bringing me home?"

Josh shook his head, and Ashley said her goodbyes. Josh thanked Andrew and Lori for allowing him to join them. Kneeling onto the snow, he accepted a big hug from Christa. "It was especially nice to meet you, Christa. I hope Santa is very good to you."

Waving goodbye, Josh and Ashley were on their own. With the exuberance, Josh was beginning to expect from her, Ashley convinced Josh to go downtown. As he drove, Ashley slid her hand across the console and clasped his, "You were really good with Christa."

"She's adorable. You have a wonderful family."

"I could tell they liked you," Ashley gleamed and then added, "I bet you are an amazing dad."

"I don't know, I have a wonderful daughter. She's my best friend, that makes it easy," Josh replied modestly, as he slipped the sedan into a space along the curb. The downtown market was bustling with people ignoring the chilly wind that had begun to funnel in through the valley. Sidewalks flowed with late-night shoppers, couples walking to and from restaurants, families admiring the storefronts.

As Josh and Ashley strolled along the street, he turned to face her, "Thank you for inviting me along."

"I'm glad you came."

"Sorry, I was a late, surprise guest."

"A welcome surprise. You can surprise me like that anytime," Ashley crooned.

At the base of the towering town square Christmas tree, a sextet of carolers treated passersby to a chorus of O Holy Night. As much as Ashley revered the traditional holiday songs, she could tell that Josh became slightly despondent, even if only briefly.

"You don't like Christmas much," Ashley observed.

Looking away for a moment, Josh licked his lips and let out a breath. Turning to face his date completely, "It's not that I don't like Christmas. I love Christmas. I love everything about it, but…"

Josh paused, chewing on his lip as he sorted through the words he wanted to share, "…but it's hard without Kaya. This used to be our favorite time together, now it is one of the longest stretches without each other. I can't stand a day without her, never mind the season that represents family the most. I love Christmas. I just don't like it without my daughter." His eyes worked their way from Ashley and focused in on the star shining high atop the tree.

"That must be hard," Ashley sympathized.

"It is. It's the worst."

"And all I have done since we met was drag you from one holiday thing to the next. I am so sorry," Ashley said earnestly.

"Don't be. People are supposed to embrace the holidays. I'm happy for them. I just usually hide from it. This is the first time that I have been home for the holidays since Kaya's mom and I divorced," Josh confided.

"You spend the holidays alone?"

"Kind of. I usually work through them, keep myself busy until I get to pick Kaya up from the airport," he admitted.

"I guess I can't even imagine what that must be like. You obviously love Kaya very much. She's lucky to have you for a Dad."

"I'm lucky to have her for a daughter," Josh corrected.

For a few moments, they studied each other silently. Their eyes searched the other's as if trying to decipher a clue as to what thoughts hid behind them. An occasional snowflake drifted between them, dancing as it fell to their feet.

"Do you want to get out of here? We can…"

"No," Josh cut her off, lightly pressing his hand against hers as if to signify that he was really okay. Suddenly he brightened as he heard the rhythmic jingle of bells marching down the street, "How about a sleigh ride?"

Ashley paused for a moment, taking in the conversation and the suggestion, hoping that she wasn't forcing him, "Are you sure?"

"Yes, I'm sure. Grinch or not, a sleigh ride on a chilly winter's night with a beautiful woman…I'm quite sure," Josh said and waved at the sleigh driver.

The driver stopped the pair of horses and waited for Josh to help Ashley into the carriage. Offering a blanket to his passengers, the driver set his team off for the park that snaked through the center of town. The combination of the sleigh bells, the soft snow that had been falling, and the warmth of being with someone that was proving to be so special made Josh feel blessed. For the first time, he was genuinely happy to be on the mainland.

"Are you always this way?" Josh asked softly.

"What way?" Ashley asked, her voice ringing of suspicion.

"So radiantly cheery, so infectiously happy and excited…"

"No," Ashley replied flatly, "Only when I meet someone that I want so much to understand, to get to know. I see the same things in you. They remain veiled most of the time, but find their way out. Like when you talk about Kaya."

Josh took a deep breath, his head suddenly a dizzying haze, his eyes helplessly drawn into Ashley's. Leaning slightly forward, he saw Ashley's lips part. Such a natural act, almost instinctively, Josh allowed his lips to meet hers. Together, they embraced - soft, delicate. Josh felt as the whole carriage had begun to spin, his body circling hers. Pulling away, their eyes locked on the other's. In silence, they pondered the moment, their eyes searching for answers inside the other's soul. In concert, they leaned in to reunite their lips, still soft but laden with heightened conviction.

Releasing, Ashley snuggled even closer under the blanket. Both once more aware of the carriage ride, the winding lighted trail of the park, and the soft falling snowflakes that lit upon them as their driver hummed softly to his horses. Josh delicately wiped a melting flake off of Ashley's nose with his thumb.

Ashley looked at Josh, seemingly hesitant before speaking, "You know, it's snowing where Kaya is right now. Christmas is like the snow, the stars…the moon trying to peek out of that cloud right there." She pointed at the sliver of moonlight peeking through the sky, "Christmas is all around you. The same Christmas that your daughter is living right now, is the same Christmas that is here with you right now."

Josh watched the light from the moon break through, casting shards of light on the snow-frosted rolling lawns of the park. He fought for words that refused to come. Instead, he leaned to Ashley with a kiss, hoping that would share that he understood her. With an arm around her shoulders, he pulled in he in close for the remainder of the sleigh ride. When the driver pulled to a stop, Josh swiftly handed the man a wad of bills and thanked him.

Helping Ashley out of the carriage, he led her back to the tree where the carolers were singing their finale - the Carol of the Bells. Arm in arm, the two listened to the sextet. When the last line echoed into the night, the singers bowed to the audience and began to gather their things. As the crowd quickly dispersed, despite a few stragglers, Josh and Ashley felt like the only ones left in the marketplace. Leaning against the split rail fence lining the walk, they remained, cuddling as though the recital was still underway. They did not want the evening to end, ignoring the empty square.

"Thank you for the evening," Josh finally whispered lightly.

Snuggling against his chest, Ashley returned, "Thank you."

Each with an arm around the other's waist, they meandered back to Josh's borrowed sedan. As he accepted directions from Ashley, Josh's mind was churning, piecing together Ashley's words and his feelings, his sadness being without Kaya and his family's caring for him. His emotions were a confused jumble of excitement, shame, fear. Pulling up to Ashley's house, he brightened, "Are you free tomorrow?"

Ashley smiled, "I am."

"I was wondering if you would help me with some Christmas loose ends."

"I'd be glad to," Ashley gave Josh a quick kiss. Before she could pull the handle of her door, Josh had jumped out and jogged around the car to open the door for her. Graciously accepting the offer, Ashley waited, giggling softly.

Hand in hand, they ambled up to her front steps—neither in a hurry to reach their inevitable destination.

Stopping shy of her doorstep, Josh squeezed her hand, "Noon tomorrow?"

Ashley nodded and spun to face him. For a long breathless moment, they stared at each other, drinking in the twilight moments of their date. Ashley pulled lightly at the collar of Josh's jacket, pulling his lips toward her own. Closing her eyes, she allowed her sense of touch to dominate her. When she opened them, she whispered, "Goodnight."

Josh took a step back. Waiting for her to turn the key and open her door, he accepted one last big smile from Ashley before returning to the car.

"Hi daddy," Kaya's voice whispered into the phone, "I was waiting for you to call."

"You sound sleepy, baby. I couldn't wait to call you. How was your day?" Josh asked.

"Great. I played with my cousins and saw grandpa and grandma. They say 'hi' by the way."

"Tell them I said hello. How are they doing?"

"They're good," Kaya replied, "Grandpa says it's not as fun without you around."

"Tell him I say the same."

"How was your day, Daddy?"

"I had a very nice day," Josh answered. He relayed the day at the farm with the reindeer. Almost feeling nervous, he fought for the words to talk about his evening, "This evening I met a friend. We actually won a prize at a snowman contest. I wish you were there."

"Me too. It sounds like you had fun. I'm glad. You should have fun even when I am not there, you know," Kaya declared flatly.

"It's easier when we are together."

"I know. But like you always tell me, you gotta try…"

Josh chuckled at his daughter's logic and reversal of parental advice. He wasn't prepared for the astute foresight that came next.

"Tell Ashley I said 'hi'. I hope I get to meet her?"

Josh stared into the phone as Kaya repeated, "She's your friend you met, right, Daddy?"

Chuckling again, Josh affirmed, "Yes. Yes, she is."

"She's the one that makes you happy," Kaya stated.

"She certainly gets me to have fun," Josh admitted.

"Will you see her tomorrow?" Kaya asked.

"I think so."

"Good. Definitely tell her I said 'hi'," Kaya demanded.

"I will, Pumpkin," Josh promised, "Now go get some sleep; I'll call you tomorrow night."

Hanging up the phone, Josh chuckled to himself. Sometimes he wondered who the parent was. As much as he took care of his daughter, he realized she did a fair job of taking care of him too.

Kaya's words hung in his mind. Their conversation, so simple on the surface, resounded in him. The frankness of Kaya's assessment of his mood, the perceptiveness that his daughter had simply by listening to him over the phone, seemed more astute and clear than his own jumbled thoughts. As he leaned against the windowsill, tracing the moonlight on the snow-covered lawn, he thought, maybe Kaya was right.

Collapsing on the pullout bed, he shut his eyes. Feeling as though the room was spinning, images of his daughter took turns in the movie reel of his mind, sharing the space occasionally with Ashley. He could still smell her on the collar of his shirt. He felt like he could still feel the touch of her lips against his. His guarded and protected heart felt very open, very vulnerable, yet curiously willing.

Chapter Nine

After breakfast, Josh tried to make his escape from the family as inconspicuous as possible. An ever-alert Sarah thwarted his attempt. "Uncle Josh! Where are you going?"

"I suppose my saying I have a few last-minute Christmas errands is beginning to run a bit thin, but it really is true today," Josh answered.

"Hmm, need any help, little brother?" Amy asked, a suspicious eyebrow raised.

"No. Thank you, I have it covered."

"You have it covered as you can handle it, or you already have help?" Amy offered a sly grin.

Refusing the bait to intensify the inquisition, Josh stated simply, "I will see you all later. You plan to still hang at the house today?"

Amy nodded and handed her brother a to-go mug of coffee. "You behave yourself, little brother."

"I will, you guys have a good day, I'll see you a bit later," Josh offered and planted kisses on the cheeks of his niece and nephew.

As Josh turned to head for the hallway, a voice called from behind, stopping him once more in his tracks. "Where are you going, Josh?"

Rolling his eyes and releasing a slight sigh, Josh pivoted on his heel and returned to the kitchen, "Good morning, mother. I was just telling Amy and the kids that I have the last of Christmas errands to complete."

"Oh, good, do you want some company?" Carol asked, filling up her coffee mug, looking at her son with hopeful eyes.

"While I very much appreciate that Mom, I think I'll do this on my own," Josh walked to his mother's side and planted a kiss on her cheek.

"Well, alright," his mother conceded, her tone suggesting a bit of disappointment.

Winking at the kids spooning oatmeal into their mouths, Josh once more wheeled towards the door. As he neared the foyer, he heard his father's voice call out, "Where's Josh going?"

Pausing with his hand on the doorknob, Josh started to face his family once more. To his relief, he heard Amy's voice ring, "I got it, Josh! You go take care of what you need!"

Finally, free from his family's well-intended curiosity, he was behind the wheel, steering his father's car toward Ashley's house. He was surprised by the butterflies that appeared in his stomach. These were a very different sort than the ones that he had experienced en route to meet her before. These had nothing to do with nervousness. These instead were lighter, they told of excitement, anticipation. Josh shook his head; he hadn't experienced feelings like this in a long time. The closest to excited butterflies, was each day when he waited for Kaya at school.

Josh was very taken aback by his head, his heart's reaction to this woman. Attractive, personable, fun, intelligent…but his feelings were almost subconscious, a natural development that seemed to be beyond his control. Had they been conscious, he reasoned, he likely would have expelled them, as he had every other woman who had displayed interest over the years. Ashley was different. She was infectious, her image, her smiley persona taking root in parts of him that had been touched only by his family.

As he pulled alongside her house, the butterflies heightened their activity, but as she stepped out onto her porch, he couldn't help but to offer a smile. The picture of her, walking steadily towards him, was almost humbling. She was beautiful, and she was confident, two attributes that were genuine inside of her and out. His quick strides caught her just as she reached the walk at the bottom of her steps, pausing to receive a hug as Ashley presented wide open arms. Grasping her hand, he walked her to the car.

The short drive to downtown, Josh took over the conversation with his captive beauty. He inquired about Ashley's traditions around the holiday and what the rest of her family was like. Ashley seemed to enjoy the relative change in roles as most of their visits had consisted of being the inquisitive one, drawing Josh out. She was glad to share pieces of her history and how important the holidays were to her. Her cheeks wore a more crimson hue as the focal of the conversation, more out of excitement of Josh's interest as opposed to discomfort in sharing.

Before they knew it, they were strolling along the familiar sidewalks of the downtown market. Arm in arm, Ashley pressing her body slightly into his, they walked the streets, selecting the proper stores in which to carry out their mission.

"Thanks for coming with me today," Josh said, admiring how attractive his shopping date was. Ashley had her white winter coat over a shapely cashmere sweater and a pair of jeans. A simple outfit, but to Josh, she looked like she had stepped out of a magazine. The crisp December breeze nipped at her cheeks, giving her the glow of a slight blush. Her chestnut hair was a flattering accent against the stark white of her coat. Josh could not have been more impressed with the beautiful woman who graced his side.

The life of the downtown market had a different feel in the day than the evening. At night, the scene was cozy with patrons bundled up, slowly taking in the lights of the Christmas tree and rows of winter-bare cherry trees that lined either side of the streets. During the day, the shoppers mixed with businessmen, each scurrying to their next destination. Josh and Ashley's pace mirrored theirs of the previous night. Slow, calm, contented.

The shops each had their own cozy appeal, working as a community to present the Twelve Days of Christmas. Their vast windows adorned with flocking and frost, framing a snapshot reflective of the holidays. Santa Clause carefully placing packages under a tree, children reaching on their tiptoes to hang their stockings on a mantle - each store offering one of the dozen scenes of the Twelve Days of Christmas, each as charming as the last. The feel of Christmas seemed to draw Ashley even closer to Josh as they strolled arm in arm down the sidewalk.

"Tell me more about Kaya, she sounds exceptional," Ashley asked as they walked.

"She is. She is so much fun," Josh beamed, "Oh, she made a point to make sure I tell you she said 'hello'."

"Well tell her 'hello' back," Ashley giggled, as the two paused to watch a mechanical elf place the star atop a tree in one of the windows, she pressed, "What does she like to do?"

"Anything to do with the water…"

"Which is good; because you live on an island," Ashley interjected and laughed, "I'm sorry, carry on."

Shooting her a playful look of mock disdain, he continued, "She loves to swim, surf, kayak, snorkel. Her favorite is cataloging all of the creatures she can find along the reefs. When we're not in the water, she has us watching shows about animals on T.V." Josh paused for a moment, smiling as he thought of his daughter, "Oh, and she and I cook. She loves finding cooking shows and making me try to make what the people on T.V. are making."

"Does that work?"

"Sometimes. We always have a back up just in case," Josh admitted.

"I love watching and listening to you talk about Kaya. You absolutely light up," Ashley admired, "Your passion and devotion for your daughter is…well, it's very attractive."

Shrugging, Josh asserted, "I just love my child. I guess I would imagine all parents are the same."

"Not that I am an expert on parenting, but I would say no. Not all parents have such commendable focus on their children," Ashley paused and then cast a scrutinizing glance, "How about you? What does Josh like to do for fun?"

"I don't know. I like volunteering at the school. And like Kaya, I love being on the ocean too. I feel at peace when I'm out there. There's something about it - powerful and undaunted. No matter what's going on in life, watching the waves roll in puts it into perspective just how insignificant our struggles are," Josh replied, "What about you? Other than assaulting customers with lattes, what do you like to do?"

"Ouch, I thought we were past that," Ashley laughed at the ribbing, "I like to explore. Whether it's around here hiking or traveling, I can't help but wonder what's around the next corner."

She paused and looked deep into Josh's eyes. Her gaze was serious and intense for a moment and then lightened, "I love

Christmas. I love everything about it. I love the story about baby Jesus and the stories of strangers traveling miles to bring gifts to a baby boy they didn't know. The idea of peace on earth. Every Christmas Eve, after church, I love how silent the world seems to get. There seems to be the one night each year that nearly everyone stops what they're doing in life. For one night, there is hope."

Josh suddenly started looking over Ashley's shoulder with a funny look on his face. "What?" Ashley asked.

"I keep expecting Jimmy Stewart to come down the street…" his voice trailed off as he received a punch on the arm from Ashley. "I guess I deserved that one."

"I try to share, and you pick on me," Ashley snapped in mock anger.

"Sorry, sorry. I appreciate that you love Christmas that much. I guess I used to too. Maybe even more."

"And now you're George Bailey standing on the bridge? Come on. You think avoiding Christmas makes it all go away? Or maybe, just maybe, you're missing a special time with others that love you, like your family. Maybe friends. You have friends, right?" Ashley retorted.

"I have friends."

"You're a wonderful man. I can see how much being without Kaya tears at you. Do you think she wants you to be this way? Or worse, that it takes a little bit away from her Christmas?" Ashley asked and then suddenly backed off, "I'm sorry. I don't mean to…"

"No, its okay," Josh shook her off, "You're right. I thought about what you told me last night. The same Christmas that you and I are living is the same Christmas that surrounds Kaya across town. I guess, I have chosen not to be a part of that. Thank you for helping me see…" Josh's voice trailed off, and his lips touched hers in a soft, brief kiss.

"I'm going to have to scold you more often," Ashley whispered, pushing on her tiptoes to meet his lips more square.

Josh grabbed her hand, "Come on, we've got work to do."

"What is our mission today?" Ashley asked.

"Well, I had presents sent to my parent's house that I had ordered online, but I have realized they are a bit uninspired. Spending time with my family, especially my sister's kids – Noah and Sarah, I want to make them a little more special. They deserve that."

"Wow, not very Grinchy of you, Mr. Daniels," Ashley teased.

Ignoring her comment, Josh gave her a curious look, "What was your favorite Christmas present?" He pushed open the door to a toy shop and held it for her.

"As a kid or an adult?"

"Any. Favorite of all time," Josh replied.

"Gosh, I have to think about that for a minute. No, I don't," Ashley suddenly snapped to attention, "I was sixteen. My father bought me my first real piece of jewelry – a beautiful ring, white gold, in the center was a space for one of a dozen little spheres that fit inside. Each ball was a different color. They were made of glass, I think, like marbles. I loved that ring. That was my last Christmas before my Dad passed." Ashley grew quiet for a moment, her eyes fixing on a blank spot on the ceiling as she reflected.

"I'm sorry," Josh whispered, placing a hand on her arm.

"It was years ago. Happy memories," Ashley smiled and then drifted again, "I wish I knew what happened to that ring…it disappeared on one of my moves to or from college."

"That's too bad. It sounds like it was special."

Shrugging, Ashley announced, "Enough about memory lane. We have new memories to create. Tell me about Noah and Sarah!"

Josh smiled, holding Ashley's hand as they peered through the aisles of toys in front of them. Something about her energy, her genuine passion for life filled him with such warmth when she was around. She somehow encouraged similar excitement in him. An enthusiasm that, with the singular exception of being a dad, had escaped some time ago. Lost for a moment in the sparkle that danced around her brilliant blue eyes, he began to describe his niece and nephew.

From store to store, Josh and Ashley scanned the aisles, adding more and more packages to their bundle. Each gift prompted Ashley to wrench a story about who was going to receive it. She would ponder a few minutes and then yank Josh by the arm in wild haste to a new store or section. The flurry of shopping yielded several trips to unload packages into the trunk of the car before returning to the shops for more.

An exhausted Josh turned to his shopping partner, "I'm not sure bringing you along was a great idea after all. I'm going to be broke."

"But you're making spirits bright, that's what matters," Ashley grinned, refusing his sarcasm, "Who do we have left?"

Josh paused, going through his mental list, "I think we have just about everyone. I wouldn't mind finding one more thing for Kaya. Something special that she can keep. Your father has inspired me."

"Nice thinking, Dad. Hmm… let me see…something special…," her eyes lit up. "I know the perfect place! The Uncommon Gift!"

"Well, it certainly sounds like the right place."

"How about jewelry, I remember seeing this adorable charm bracelet there. That way, you two can add to it with all of your favorite things or places. That way, it's like a story you can build on," Ashley suggested.

"I think you have outdone yourself. That is a brilliant idea," Josh declared and was excitedly pulling Ashley towards the gift shop. Once inside, they were quickly greeted by the owner, who brought them to a gleaming display of charm bracelets. Selecting one that Josh felt matched his daughter's personality, they turned their attention to the charms. There were so many to choose from that it could have been overwhelming. However, one in particular stood out to Josh; without hesitation, he made his purchase.

Back out on the sidewalk, Ashley linked her arm in Josh's. Taking one last stroll through the square, they took in the Christmas music, the haste of frantic shoppers, the Salvation Army bell intermingled with calls of "Merry Christmas", all blending wonderfully with the crisp December air. For the first time all season, Josh seemed to notice it all, appreciate it all. He gently pulled Ashley by their linked arms closer. The move met in silence, but the glowing smile Ashley provided spoke loud.

With a trunk full of packages, Josh pulled into Ashley's driveway. Once more rushing around the car, he held open her door and escorted her up the steps to her porch. The sun had broken through the clouds and radiated down on top of them. Ashley's chestnut hair shone as though glossed with metallic paint. The light highlighted the freckles that danced along her nose, enhancing her already radiant eyes, causing their deep mahogany to seem as though they could seep all the way into her vibrant soul. Josh felt overwhelmingly consumed with admiration, attraction for her.

Ashley's sparkling eyes met with his, "I had fun today!"

Rejecting the initial sarcastic jab about how fun it is to spend someone else's money, he relented to his true feelings instead, "I did too. I'm glad you came with me."

Standing on her tiptoes, she gave Josh a firm, passionate kiss. Watching him descend her steps to his car, she smiled and whispered to herself, "And the Grinch's heart grew three sizes that day…"

As Josh clambered into the house with his first of several trips full of packages, the entire family paused at what they were doing to gape at his bounty. Ignoring their stares, he ran back to the car for another load. Finally, carrying the last of the presents into the den, he shrugged as he passed their questioning looks. Without a word, he joined his family, who was still staring in silence at his return. Sliding the presents for the kids that he had wrapped at the store under the tree, he turned to face his family. "What?" he asked innocently.

Josh was not surprised when his sister was the first to speak up. "I need to meet the woman who finally got to Scrooge," she chortled.

"Josh met someone?" his mother broke in.

"Way to go, Josh!" Bob called from the kitchen.

"So, tell us all the details, little brother," Amy said, curling her legs under her as she looked on with anticipation.

"I went shopping," Josh said nonchalant, "I told you I had a few last-minute things to do."

"Last minute? I don't think Santa himself puts that much last minute stuff together, besides your usual shipment of presents had already arrived," his dad pressed.

"I know. I figured I'm here; I wanted to make it more special. Who could resist with these two?" Josh grinned, pulling Noah and Sarah into a giant bear hug.

"Humph, I'll get the truth out of you, little brother," Amy warned.

"So," Josh said curtly, rubbing his hands together, "What does a guy have to do around here for a cookie and some eggnog?"

"Would you grab another jug from the fridge in the garage?" Carol asked.

"Sure."

"And one of those holiday beers…," Nick called from the living room.

"Sure, Dad! Anything else anybody needs?" Josh asked, poking his head in the living room, studying the faces.

"Will you play with us when you come back in?" Noah called out.

"You bet!" Josh answered and disappeared into the garage.

As he poked his head in the refrigerator, he pulled out a jug of eggnog and then began shuffling through his father's collection of holiday grog, searching for the seasonal stout that had impressed him this year. From behind, he could hear the garage door creak open and the shuffling of clippers on the concrete floor.

"Hey, little brother, hand me one of the lighter beers," Amy requested. With his free hand, Josh grasped two beers by the neck, handing one to his sister.

Popping the bottle open, Amy unfolded a step ladder that had been leaning against a post and sat down on a rung. Seeing his sister's intent, he sat down the eggnog and the bottle of beer he grabbed for Nick. Reaching back into the fridge, he retrieved a beer for himself. "Yes?" he asked, a suspicious tone in his question.

"I just want to see how you are really doing. You certainly seem happy, Amy confided, though her countenance declared her obvious underlying concern.

"I'm good. Thanks for the assist this morning night with Mom, by the way."

"No problem, I'm here for you," Amy replied, and then pressed, "So, tell me about your friend."

Josh hesitated for a moment, then looking at his sister's expectant affect, knew she would not relent, "She is nice. A lot of fun, full of energy. She almost pulls me along, but in a demanding way. In a way that seems illogical to resist. She is very much a free spirit, yet sophisticated…"

"Wow, little brother. I haven't heard you talk about anybody like that since…," Amy began and then realized the sensitivity of her conclusion.

"I know," Josh broke in, his voice belying the same concern that she apparently held.

"She sure has gotten you to open up about Christmas," Amy observed.

Josh nodded, "She has a way of reaching within me and yanking things out. Without telling me, or leading me…she just asks questions in a way that forces me to dig a little deeper within myself. She changes the way that I see everything around me. I can't really explain…"

"Whoa, Josh Daniels, that is deep. You know, I'm glad. Happy looks good on you…," Amy paused as she swallowed a gulp of her beer, "I worry about you getting too close."

"What do you mean?" Josh asked warily.

"What happens when you leave?"

"I…I don't know," Josh shrugged, "I am just enjoying myself now. I'm not applying any expectations or labels on where we are or where we are going. Like you said, she has definitely opened me up to enjoy the holidays. Not that I haven't enjoyed being with the family, let's face it, the holidays themselves have been a bit of a challenge for me."

"I know. I can see that. It's taken you so long to even look at another woman, I'm nervous for you getting attached to one that you are going to leave behind," Amy considered, "Or, is that part of it? You know you are leaving."

"Trust me, Sis, there is no planning on my part. She worked her way in. I'm not sure how. I'm not sure I care. I suppose it is a little exciting, a little frightening all at the same time. I'll be alright," Josh conceded.

Amy sat thoughtfully nursing her beer, "Good. I won't press you any more. I'm happy for you. I just wanted to make sure you were okay." Rising off of the step ladder, she threw her arms around her brother and pulled him into a sincere hug.

"Thanks, Sis."

"You'll always be my baby brother," Amy admitted, and then abruptly changing the mood, "Now let's see about those cookies!"

Kneeling on the floor, Josh joined Noah and Sarah as they played with the train that circled his mother's Christmas village. The kids had set up several stops for their "elves" to manage their pre-Christmas duties. Sarah handed Josh a little stuffed bear figure to put on the train on its way to Santa's workshop.

Amy winked at him from above her cup of cocoa. She loved seeing him interact with her kids. He had always been the one to crawl along the floor and get to their level. Her kids were always excited for an "Uncle Josh visit".

For hours, Josh devoted himself to enjoying the company of his niece and nephew. From completing the elf missions to helping color a massive Toyland color page to assembling a puzzle that depicted Santa's reindeer skidding to a stop on the peak of a rooftop.

Amy and Carol huddled on the couch, nudging each other as they watched the kids with their uncle. They hadn't spoken much of Josh's holiday transformation, but they both appreciated what they were witnessing.

"Mom had some shopping to do without me, so I stayed home with Roger. We played Chutes and Ladders and Candy Land, and then he started teaching me how to play chess. That will take some work. Do you know how to play chess, Daddy?" Kaya asked into the phone.

Josh sat on the swing in the backyard, slowly wobbling back and forth as he talked his daughter, "Yes, I know how. We'll have to break out my set when we get home. It is nice that Roger took the time to teach you, it requires a lot of patience."

"Yeah, it's not like playing with you. You and I do exciting stuff, but Roger's more into quieter, brainy stuff. It's okay. Did you see Ashley today?"

"Yes, I did…" Josh started before Kaya jumped in.

"Did you tell her I said 'hello'?" she demanded.

"Yes. She says 'hello' back."

"I think I like her. Do you like her daddy?" Kaya asked bluntly.

"Yes, I do like her," Josh admitted, "She makes me see things in a different way, a good way."

"How's that?" Josh could tell Kaya had a confused tone in her voice.

"Sometimes people, especially dads, can forget what is really important. We think we know, but then we get distracted with work and life. Ashley reminds me of what is important," he relayed.

"How does she do that?"

"By loving life in every way. She is like a kid at Christmas…"

"You used to be like that, Daddy!" Kaya exclaimed.

"I know," Josh answered softly, kicking at the snow in front of the swing, "I miss you, Kaya."

"I miss you too, Daddy. I wish you were with me."

"Me too, sweetheart. Me too," Josh replied, and then his voice brightened, "Can you go to the window? Look out at the stars. You know what? I see the same ones."

"You do?" Kaya gasped.

"I sure do. See that one star that is a little brighter than all the rest?"

"Uhhh… there it is. I see it!"

"No matter where we are, we are always under the same stars. I love you, honey."

"I love you too, Daddy."

Chapter Ten

Even for an adult who had largely rejected the holiday, Josh awoke the morning of Christmas Eve, feeling the energetic buzz in the air. He could already hear Noah and Sarah excitedly chattering while waiting for their breakfast. Knowing that his mother and sister would hold breakfast for him, he hastened down the hallway to join his family in the kitchen. Bob and his dad hadn't made their way in yet, so Josh made a line for the coffee pot to pour the last cup before making another batch. In front of the stove, Josh's mother was just sliding the first batter-dipped French toast into a sizzling skillet. The aroma of bacon quickly began to take over the kitchen, whetting Josh's appetite.

Sliding into a seat beside Noah, he took a big gulp of coffee. "Are you excited?" he asked.

"I can't hardly wait for tomorrow Uncle Josh," his milk-mustached nephew admitted.

"Me neither," Sarah chimed and politely added, "I like Christmas Eve too. Everyone stops working. The presents are ready…all we have to do is play games and watch more Christmas movies."

Josh chuckled and commended his niece, "I like that you appreciate what you have before you. That is very Aloha of you."

"She doesn't get that from her mother," the patriarch of the family grumbled through a sleepy, non-caffeinated voice, "Amy was horrible at birthdays and Christmas, always snooping and shaking packages trying to figure what she got."

"What about Uncle Josh? What was he like?" Sarah asked.

"He was patient. He liked surprises. Mostly, I think he was so careful to maintain tradition. I think he thought if he snuck and found out what his presents were, he would ruin Christmas," his mother added.

"Ruin Christmas?" Noah gasped.

"You can't really ruin Christmas, Noah," Josh consoled, "It is much bigger than presents or decorations or any of those things. It's more about being with family and, of course, baby Jesus."

Amy spun and stared at her brother, spatula in hand, "What in the world has gotten into you, Mr. Bah Humbug, I'll stay on the island and work? You sound more like a Norman Rockwell painting come to life."

"Or Linus from Peanuts," Bob added sleepily from the doorway.

"I don't care who he sounds like, it's nice. Besides, he's right," his mother defended.

"Aahhh, you always took his side!" Amy taunted in mock irritation.

"I was the good kid!" Josh teased back, "So does anyone need anything from town today?"

"You're leaving again?" Sarah looked at her uncle with disappointment.

"For a little while. I promised a friend."

"Mom says you always need to keep your promises," Sarah nodded sullenly.

"Your Mom is right on that one. I'll be back this afternoon to hang with you guys," Josh said, and then winked, "That's a promise."

When Josh arrived at the coffee shop, the festivities were in full swing. A Santa Clause stood in front of the shop, greeting guests and waving at children, handing out candy canes to those who came within reach. A large crowd had amassed, and Josh had struggled to squeeze through and get to the counter. Behind the bar, a half-dozen of Ashley's employees toiled to keep up with the demand, though each seemed more than happy to be there.

Ashley paused when she saw Josh, freezing in place with a tray of Christmas cookies in her hand. Her eyes brightened, and she gave Josh a huge smile, "You ready to work?"

"I am," Josh admitted.

"Then come on back, you can hang your coat on a hook," biting her lip, she looked thoughtful for a moment and added, "You can put those sales skills of yours to work offering up these cookies."

Josh hung his coat and entered the crowd with the tray. At first, the group of mostly orphans and foster children along with the social workers who brought them were hesitant until Josh insisted, "Come on guys, you have to help me, I won't be allowed to return with a full tray of cookies, and I don't know how long my arm can hold out."

One little girl with wild, curly hair accepted, her big blue eyes looking straight at Josh's. He could see the immense gratitude well from within her as though he were giving her the greatest gift ever. He reasoned that she was not used to receiving much of anything from anyone. Suddenly, Josh felt as though he had been given the best job ever. With inspired exuberance, he embraced his duties of dolling out the holiday cookies.

The smiles on each child's face melted his heart; joy filled him in a way that could only be rivaled by his daughter. As the plate of cookies was quickly emptied, Josh spied the social workers pooled in the back of the shop, yielding to the kids. Making his way over, he encouraged them to participate, "Come on, the cookies taste good to adults, too! Can we get you a latte or cocoa?"

Like the children, the social workers hesitated until one brave soul accepted. Soon, Josh had a large order to be filled and an empty tray. Wading his way back through the giggling swarm of children, he returned to the counter. Ashley saw him out of the corner of her eye and grinned, her eyes sparkling as she spoke, "You are really good out there!"

Shrugging, Josh nodded towards the happy throng of kids, "How could I not? This is wonderful. Oh, I hope it's okay; I took an order from the social workers who brought them."

"Of course. We offered when they first got here, but they declined in favor of the kids. I'm glad you got them to feel welcome. Without them, we wouldn't have the kids here, would we?"

As the drinks were made, Josh delivered them himself as the kids were distracted by Santa Clause passing out presents. Ashley had received all of their names and an idea of what each child liked. Collecting donations since Thanksgiving, she was able to provide a gift for each child. Through the murmur, Josh could hear how excited the kids were that Santa knew their names.

Sitting on the edge of a table, he passed out the drinks to the social workers. "You have incredible jobs," he remarked.

"Bittersweet at the same time, I suppose," one of the ladies remarked.

"Some days, it's the best. Helping a child into a better situation or family," another chimed in, "Other's it is incredibly hard. This time of year, we ride a fine line. It's exciting, we decorate with them, make gifts for their foster families, but we can also see how heartbreakingly lonely they get as well. Especially the closer to Christmas Day they get."

"It's great that you guys put this on each year. It's wonderful to see the kids' faces when they see that Santa Clause remembers them and that people like the staff here care," another social worker added.

"I'm just here to help for the day," Josh admitted, "Frankly, I'm honored to be here."

They all paused as they watched the kids open their presents. A mix of emotions washed over the room. Cheers and excitement over the gifts, kids taking dolls and cars, and stuffed bears out of their packaging. For a few, there were confused tears. They were overwhelmed with happiness and yet pained with the rare touch of caring that they had so seldom received.

Josh's throat tightened, his eyes moving from child to child, taking in the scene. As the group had gathered their toys, dusted cookie crumbs off of their clothes, and thanked Santa, the social workers thanked Josh and the staff for hosting the event. Josh was surprised to feel a light patting against his leg. He turned to find the little girl with curly hair looking up at him. Her familiar doe eyes intently peering into his own. The lump in Josh's throat expanded as he knelt to receive a hug from her as she thanked him.

Fighting a tear that surprised him as it welled up, he pulled away and looked at her. "What's your name? I'm Josh," he said and held out his hand.

Shaking it with exuberance, she responded in a tiny squeaky voice, "My name's Nella."

"Well, Nella, it's a pleasure to meet you. Thank you for coming."

"Thank me?" she asked, bewildered.

"Yes, meeting you is a gift that I did not expect this year," casting a glance towards Ashley who was shaking hands with the social worker staff, he added, "I've had a couple of those this year."

"It was nice to meet you, Mr. Josh."

"Merry Christmas, Nella," Josh said softly, giving her a last quick hug and steered her back to the group.

As the last child filtered out, the crew quickly set to cleaning the shop and returning it to its normal function. Ashley thanked her staff and passed out cards and gifts to them all. Two employees volunteered to work the closing shift allowing those with families to go home. Hanging her own apron up, she made a pair of cappuccinos and grabbed a plate of breads, nodding to Josh to join her at a table in the corner.

"Thanks for coming," Ashley smiled.

"Are you kidding me? This was terrific. Do you do this every year?" Josh asked.

"Since we opened. This is our third year," Ashley nodded, "You were quite a hit. With the adult ladies and the little curly-haired girl."

"Didn't notice the ladies, but Nella – that's the curly-haired girl, was very sweet," Josh admitted.

"She was a cutie," Ashley said over her coffee cup and let out a mischievous grin, "She has good taste too."

Josh just rolled his eyes as he played the foam around the top of his cappuccino.

"You are very good with kids," Ashley said admiringly, "And not so bad with adults either." Placing her hand on the table, she offered it to Josh, who joined his hand in hers.

Shrugging, Josh answered humbly, "I love kids. I have the best time with Kaya and her friends. I volunteer at her school whenever I can, helping out at Field Day or field trips."

"She's lucky to have a father like you."

"I don't know. I just do what I figure most parents should. We only get a limited number of precious years with our kids. I try not to waste a moment. You're not so bad with them yourself. Do you miss teaching?" Josh turned the tables.

"I do. Like you, I find ways to stay involved. I pick up substitution gigs when I can. The school is good to me," Ashley replied, "So what is it like? Living in Hawaii?"

"I love it. Aside from missing seasons, it's wonderful. Once you are acclimated and obviously adopting the 'aloha' lifestyle, the locals are very accepting. Kaya and I find ourselves groaning about the mainlanders as much as they do. What can I say, it's paradise. It truly is," Josh shrugged.

"Does that make you no longer a 'haole'?"

"No, we'll always be haolies, but the folks in our town have accepted us. It's just a matter of fitting into their culture, not forcing ours. Hawaiians are great people, full of love," Josh laughed.

"Is it hard being away from your family?"

"I don't know. Kaya and I visit a couple of times a year. They have threatened to visit us there. They have an open invitation," Josh replied, "Have you ever been?"

Shaking her head, Ashley answered, "I've always wanted to. Since I bought the shop, I've been pretty well tied down."

"Big responsibility, owning your own business."

"It is. I like it. I need to learn to get away from it a bit more. I have a great team. They can easily get by without me, maybe the shop'd even run smoother," Ashley admitted.

"I think you'd be missed. I see how the community interacts with you. You are amazing."

"I don't know about that. I love this place. The people have become my family, my friends," Ashley replied meekly.

"I can see that. Probably why your downtown flourishes while others are withering – there is a real sense of community here."

"It doesn't matter if it is the Fourth of July, our First Friday events, or when someone is in need, they all come together."

"I can see why you like it," Josh nodded thoughtfully, "Still to buy a coffee shop…"

"This place was like my second home when I was a new teacher. Nights that I didn't want to go home and be alone, I'd set up shop in here, grading papers or making lesson plans. Even if I was by myself, it was nice to be surrounded by other people. I love the noises of the coffee shop, the smells, the people watching," Ashley replied, "A few years back, the owner had passed. The development firm that owns the complex wanted to find a franchise chain to put in here. But this place has been here for twenty years. It's like an institution. On a whim, I took my vested benefits and sunk them all into buying this place. My friends thought I was crazy. Maybe they were right."

"I think it's fantastic. Not many people would take such a risk, and it seems as though you've done a great job," Josh admired.

"Thank you," Ashley conceded, "It has worked out pretty well."

"Another example of what an intriguing, impressive woman you are," Josh replied.

"That is quite the compliment from you, thank you," Ashley blushed for the first time Josh could remember since he met her. Toying with the foam in the bottom of her nearly dry cappuccino, she asked, "Can you stay for a while?"

Glancing at his watch, Josh sighed and shook his head, "I promised my niece and nephew I would get back and spend the afternoon with them." Ashley nodded disappointedly. The air hung heavy for a moment, both sitting in silence. When Josh spoke, he almost surprised himself as he blurted, "Do you want to come with us to the nativity pageant tonight?"

"I…I'd love to," Ashley replied.

"I'll pick you up at seven?" Josh asked.

"That sounds perfect. Now you go spend time with your niece and nephew," she said sternly.

"Alright," Josh agreed obediently. As he got up, he grabbed their dishes and carried them back behind the counter as he grabbed his coat.

Following, Ashley nearly ran into him as he turned around. Straining on her tiptoes, she planted a soft kiss on his lips, "Thanks again for helping today."

As Josh left, he felt like he could float over the sidewalk to his car. He felt an excitement and a sense of wholeness that he hadn't felt in years. He didn't know what to make of it, but he enjoyed how it made him feel. He felt like it made him a better person to be around. He was deeply thankful, whatever it was.

Josh's mind wandered as he drove back towards his family. Helping give to the kids at the shop was an incredible experience. Meeting little Nella was undeniably heartwarming. All through the collection of images that projected in his head, one stunningly beautiful figure kept popping into frame. Ashley was so graceful, invigorating, and giving at the shop. She wore an impressive array of personas – the humble and embarrassed barista he met the first night, the playful and energetic woman who enticed him to visit the frozen falls. This calm and cool aunt had great family ties, the incredibly alluring woman who was inch by inch capturing his heart and his mind.

Shaking his head, he felt almost foolish for thinking so much about this woman he had barely met. Yet here he was, mindlessly driving down the road, terribly distracted by Ashley. The mere thought of her, the mention of her name quickened his pulse. Josh was unsure whether to laugh along with himself or curse at himself for allowing his feelings to open so.

Turning down a side street, Josh's thoughts jarred back to his current whereabouts. His eyes were flooded with the familiar drive, finding himself in front of his old house once again. The new family's Christmas tree gleamed with garland and lights through the large living room window. The snowman out front looked genuinely happy to Josh. In contrast to the startled, mixed emotions he was confronted with the first time he drove by, he somehow felt comforted that a happy family occupied the house.

Taking a deep breath as he passed by, Josh was overcome by feeling strangely content. He was okay that he, Dana, and Kaya weren't the ones living there. He was inexplicably okay that he and Dana lived half an ocean apart, and she was building a new life with Roger. Being without Kaya even for a day was never going to be a positive for Josh. The fact that his daughter's life seemed somehow less whole and less healthy by not being part of a traditional nuclear family would always bother him. Not being there to experience all of her joys and help her through the lows, even for a brief period, would always tear at him, stab his heart. Yet, he was glad that when he couldn't be there, she was in good hands.

He drove on, instead of being bitter and feeling hollow as he passed their old home, he felt thankful. Thankful that Dana gave him custody, and he was able to share most of Kaya's experiences with her. He felt a twinge of sadness for Dana in not being able to be there as much as he was.

Absentmindedly, he flipped on the radio, landing on a station playing nothing but Christmas songs. Without fully realizing it, he softly hummed happily along to each song that played until he pulled into his parent's driveway.

Amy watched her brother float through the front door. A glow seemed to radiate from him. Her mind contrasted this entrance to his appearance when he first arrived. She was thrilled to see him this way. As Josh hung up his coat, he smiled, "Hi, Sis!"

"Hello, little brother," Amy smiled back, "The kids have been waiting for you. They're in the kitchen helping make another batch of cookies, like we need more."

"Smells good, anyway."

As Josh kicked off his shoes and moved toward the kitchen, Amy blocked his path. Without saying a word, she gave him a long, hearty hug.

"I love you too, sis. I'm glad I came home," Josh said earnestly, looking into his sister's eyes.

"Me too," releasing her bear hug, she watched her brother slink off toward the kitchen to surprise her children.

Amy smiled quietly to herself as she heard the chorus of excited voices crying out, "Uncle Josh!" Studying a group of pictures clustered on a bookcase in the living room, she paused, picking up one of Josh and Kaya. The smile on her brother's face spoke aloud of his love and happiness. That is a look she had not seen on Josh in quite some time. Her heart silently ached for such a time when her deserving brother was once more filled with such contented happiness.

In the kitchen, Josh was receiving enthusiastic hugs from Sarah and Noah. The two kids left a series of flour-laced handprints all over his clothes, but he didn't mind. "Whatcha making?" he asked.

"Grandpa's cookie recipe. We're going to decorate them for Santa!" Sarah exclaimed.

"Hmmm, you trust a recipe from Grandpa?" Josh raised an eyebrow.

"Well, he got it from his mom," Noah declared.

"Then you should be fine. She was a good cook," Josh pronounced, rubbing his chin thoughtfully, "After all, if we're leaving cookies for Santa, they better be good."

Both kids stared at Josh as though they hadn't thought of that. Glancing at their grandparents with nervous, questioning looks, their grandmother asserted, "It's a good recipe. It has my seal of approval."

Sarah and Noah looked relieved as they returned to their work. "You wanna help stir, Uncle Josh?" Sarah asked as she struggled to move the large wooden spoon around the bowl.

"You bet!" Josh agreed and jumped into work with his niece and nephew in producing cookies for Santa.

Carol glanced over her work at her son, smiling approvingly to herself. She was both thrilled and relieved to see him lighthearted and engaged. Guilt over forcing him to do something he wasn't quite ready for had settled in, but by the magic of Christmas…or something appeared to have turned him around. Either way, she was glad to have her son back.

Chapter Eleven

Josh couldn't tell who was more anxious, Ashley, or himself. He pulled his father's sedan into an empty space and gave her hand a squeeze. "This should be fun," he declared, breaking the silence, his voice airing a hint of nervous sarcasm.

Ashley gave a sly smile, not giving in to his fears, "Yes, it will be. Thanks for inviting me."

"Just as a heads up, you know my family will be here," Josh winced as he studied the headliner of the car, "It's possible that Dana and her family could be here as well."

Ashley didn't flinch at Josh's warning, instead, she smiled even brighter, "Then I'll get to meet Kaya!"

Josh could not have heard a better response. Suddenly, any butterflies or concerns that danced around his heart and mind melted away. Ashley's confidence and genuine kindness always seemed to offer Josh a sense of comfortable assurance about whatever situation they had encountered. He admired her calm poise, which illuminated her voluminous inner strength. It was one of the many things he had begun to appreciate in his beautiful companion.

Opening his door, he ran around the car as Ashley had become accustomed to him doing, he slipped for a moment in the slush of the parking lot, catching himself on the hood of the car. Peering through the windshield, he gritted through a cheesy grin. Completing the circuit, he held the door and offered his hand to help Ashley out.

"You know," she said, "You are the only date who has ever opened my car door for me."

Josh stammered, trying to find an appropriate response, but could only offer a weak, shrugging smile. Ashley could see the wheels turning in Josh's head and added, "I like it. You make me feel special."

"You are," Josh replied softly, giving Ashley's hand a squeeze.

The pair navigated the parking lot, Ashley snuggling close to Josh to escape the cold wind that sang through the night. As they approached the church, it was very much the warm sanctuary that they sought. Simple white lights adorned the fir trees that dotted the sides of the building, at the very tip of the steeple, a brilliant star lit the way. Standing in the entry, a volunteer was passing out programs and candles while welcoming guests.

Once inside, Josh and Ashley shook off the chill. The church was bathed in the glow of soft lighting and flickering candles, matching the warmth the building afforded those escaping the cold. From the foyer, they could hear a piano lightly playing traditional carols as church-goers milled and mingled. Near the entry to the chapel, Josh found his family waiting. The ladies wore velvet dresses in dark green and scarlet. Sarah's dress was puffy at the bottom, encouraging her to swish her hips, causing it to swirl around her legs. The boys wore suits; Josh laughed as all three were tugging at their collars uncomfortably.

A glowing grin overtook Josh as he approached them. His hand let go of Ashley's as he gently placed it on the back of her waist. "Hey guys!" he called, tenderly guiding his date, "I'd like you to meet Ashley."

Before Josh could complete the introductions, his mother stepped in, "I'm so glad you could join us tonight. We've been wondering who captured his attention…"

Amy cut her mother off, "We are all glad to meet you. Josh is special to us, and it takes someone special to attract his attention, I think my mother was trying to say. I have to add, whatever you have done, I haven't seen him this happy in a long time."

"I feel very fortunate you have been gracious enough to let me steal him for a while this Christmas," Ashley beamed.

"I think he's been fortunate to have met you," Josh's father added.

"Ashley, it's nice to meet you," Bob said and diplomatically stated, "Now, if you are all done gushing and embarrassing them, let's find some seats." Josh shot Bob a thankful look to stop the parade of comments about him and his date.

As they followed Bob, Ashley eyed Sarah and Noah, who was studying her quietly. "You must be Noah…and you, Sarah. Josh has talked a lot about you two."

"He did?" Sarah asked, her eyes big, and her cheeks blushed.

"Yes, I think seeing you two has been the highlight of his trip back home," Ashley confirmed at the beaming pair of children.

"It has," Josh nodded as Sarah circled to his side and held his free hand.

Noah continued to look at Ashley, in apparent admiration. Amy noticed and winked at Ashley, "I think Noah likes you. He's never this quiet!"

"I am not at all surprised what a wonderful family Josh has," Ashley said as they followed Bob into a pew. The kids scrambled to sit next to Josh and his guest.

Before he sat, Josh scanned the room. He wasn't sure he would see them there, but his chest tightened as his eyes found what they had searched for. Across the aisle, a few pews back, Josh saw Dana and Roger leading Kaya to a section of seats. As Dana's eyes caught his, she leaned down and whispered into Kaya's ear. Kaya's head shot up, and an enormous grin swept across her face.

Sprinting across the aisle, Kaya zigzagged her way through the sea of legs and bodies of the church members who were filing in themselves. Josh stepped into the aisle to meet her. As he began to kneel, Kaya leaped into his arms, hooking her legs around her father's waist, "Daddy!"

"Hi baby," Josh cooed as their bear hug tightened. He drank his daughter's hug in, feeling her fill his soul.

Finally, he released her dangling feet back on the floor. With an enormous grin, she waved wildly at her relatives, "Merry Christmas!"

"Kaya, this is…," Josh began.

"I know, this is Ashley," Kaya offered a warm smile at the attractive woman and exclaimed, "You're the one that makes daddy smile. I could hear it over the phone!"

Leaning into Ashley's side, she squeezed her in a tight hug. Looking up, her eyes grew serious as she said, "Thank you."

Ashley bent down to receive the hug more fully, "I thought I saw him smile big when he talked about you. He's absolutely blissful when you are with him."

"Really happy, right? Me too," Kaya nodded.

As Ashley let her go, Kaya was enveloped by her cousins, grandparents, and aunt and uncle. Looking at Josh, Ashley watched him taking in every moment with his daughter, "She's beautiful, just like her father."

"I don't know about that," Josh whispered.

"You should see how radiant you were when you saw her coming over. It's a blessing how in love you are with your daughter," Ashley confided.

"I'm definitely blessed." Josh looked slightly crestfallen once everyone had a chance to say hello to Kaya, he knew she would have to go back with her mother. She stopped and gave her dad one more hug and a quick wave to Ashley before streaking across the aisle.

Josh mouthed a thank you to Dana as Kaya returned to her mother's side. He could see she was chattering insistently to her mother. Dana kept shaking her head 'no'. Finally, Dana looked up at Josh, who shrugged and then understanding what Kaya had been pleading, nodded, and waved them over. He could see the distressed look in Dana's eyes and returned a reassuring look. Reluctantly, she conceded and tugged Roger as she followed her gleeful daughter across the aisle.

Making room in their pew, Josh's family exchanged greetings to Dana and Roger. "Merry Christmas," Josh said, shaking Roger's hand, "Kaya has told me about all the fun she has had with you. I'm glad you're there for her."

Roger thanked him, and suddenly Dana appeared between the two. Giving Josh a quick hug, she wished him a 'Merry Christmas'. Josh introduced her to Ashley. "Kaya has told me a lot about you, at least as much as she picked up from Josh over the phone. I'm not sure how you managed to do it, but I am glad you broke through to him. Josh is a good man," Dana pronounced to Ashley and shot Josh an approving look.

"Thank you, he thinks very highly of you as well," Ashley replied, "You have a beautiful daughter."

Beaming, Dana nodded, "She is very special."

In front of the congregation, the music started, and the choir's voice rose throughout the hall. Josh thought he would feel incredibly awkward, but found himself oddly comfortable with Ashley and his family to one side and Kaya, his ex-wife and her boyfriend on the other. It seemed silly to him, but the chorus "Peace on Earth" kept ringing through his head.

Throughout the program, Josh found the words spoken by the minister and sung by the choir had an astonishing effect on him, the meaning of each especially moving. It seemed as if he never took the time to really invest in the meaning of the words and what they represented. For the last couple of years and much of this one, he had turned his back on Christmas. As the Nativity was re-enacted to the choir's hymns and the minister's messages of family and faith were shared before the crowded congregation, Josh felt a mix of shame and joy. He was ashamed for how selfish he had acted, how afraid he was to lift his head during the holidays. He realized he was afraid of what he might miss. He realized that he missed it, whether he took notice or not. He was humbled by the experience, the love of his family, the strength of a stranger to reach out, the common love – all ten years of her shared between him and the love of his past.

As Kaya wrapped herself around his left arm, Ashley lightly held his hand on the right. Josh felt as though angels surrounded him. He pictured himself pacing the lanai in Kona, trying to come with new ways to rationalize to his mother why he could not make it for the holidays again. He was very glad that she was as persistent as she was. With all of his resistance, the love he felt from his family was something he didn't realize how much he missed. He missed Kaya bitterly, true, but that didn't mean he had to ignore all others in his life that missed him too. And then there was Ashley. Like a Christmas angel, she led him back to the true meaning of the season. She found his heart layered underneath years of protective crust. He glanced at Ashley as the choir sang Carol of the Bells; the music served as mere background for Josh as he lost himself in the most profound thoughts. She was beautiful, bright, and so utterly full of life. He couldn't believe that he had barely noticed her at first.

Suddenly he was nudged as it was his turn to light his candle as the flame spread from person to person in the congregation. His gaze locked with Ashley's for a moment before touching her candle to his. As his flame took to life, the light danced magically as it reflected off of Ashley's eyes. Pausing in her light for only a moment, he gently swung to Kaya. His daughter giggled sweetly as he brought her candle aflame. Passing the flame was a beautiful ritual which came alive as member by member, the parishioners joined the choir. To Josh, Kaya's merry voice soared above the crowd. The happiness in each note carried through the chapel. Josh, feeling as blessed as he ever had, softly singing along himself.

When the song was over, the minister shared one last story and dismissed the crowd as the choir sang 'Silent Night'. Ashley whispered in Kaya's ear, both giggling as Josh faced Dana and Roger. Hugging Dana, Josh simply wished them Merry Christmas. "Thank you for joining us and sending Kaya over to say hello in the first place."

"Of course, Josh. I know you love her. She is a little lost without you," Dana replied.

"She needs you too. I'm glad you have time with her, and she's been able to get to know Roger better," Josh admitted, his words a bit more charitable than perhaps he actually felt. They were feelings he knew he had to nourish.

"We should probably get going. Merry Christmas, Josh," Dana conceded through sullen lips.

Kaya pressed her face against her dad's waist as she hugged him. Kneeling, Josh circled her cheek softly with the back of his finger, "I love you, Kaya."

"I love you too, Daddy. I'll call you tomorrow," Kaya replied, her face a conflicted twist of a smile with a twinge of sadness.

Josh watched Dana escort, Kaya, with an arm on her shoulder as the three made their way to the entrance of the church. Josh's heart felt heavy as his daughter disappeared into the crowd. Ashley squeezed his hand firmly in support. His family, too, began to make their way out of the church.

As they stepped outside into the lightly falling snow, Josh turned to his family, "I'll catch up with you guys at home."

His family nodded, and then his mother spoke up, "Ashley, I'm sure you have your own family to celebrate with, but if you would like to, we'd love for you to join us tomorrow."

Ashley was stunned momentarily. As she peered at Josh, his eyes offered his eager concurrence. "I'd love to. This is the year

Christmas is at my sister-in-law's. I hadn't decided if I was going with them yet."

"Lovely, we'll see you for breakfast then. Goodnight!" Josh's mother wisped away, leaving Josh and Ashley alone in the drifting snow.

Arm in arm, they made their way to the car. "I'm not in a hurry to take you home, if you're not in a hurry to go home," Josh stated.

"I'm not," Ashley said, her face next to his as he opened her door. For a moment, the two paused, almost suspended in time, before Ashley slid into her seat.

As Josh drove towards downtown, Ashley reflected, "Dana and Roger seem nice."

"Yeah," Josh admitted flatly.

"Kaya is everything you described…and more," Ashley continued, "She seems extraordinarily grounded and adjusted."

"Sometimes, I wondered who was helping who through the changes our lives had taken," Josh confided.

"I think you might be doing better than you have allowed yourself to realize."

Josh put the car in park. The streets and sidewalks were quiet and sparsely trafficked. All of the lights of the decorated trees and storefronts shone brightly, reflecting the snowflakes as they gently meandered to the ground. Performing his familiar circuit around the car, Josh was a bit more paced and thoughtful. Ashley looked at him with curiosity as he opened her door and helped her out. "Are you okay?" she wondered if perhaps she had pushed the conversation too far.

Josh nodded quietly as he held his hand out for her to grasp. Casually, he led Ashley on a stroll down the snow-blanketed town square walk. "I'm not sure how well-adjusted I am. Not sure where I'd be without a little help," Josh shrugged, stopping their stroll in a quiet spot on the backside of the town tree, the spot that was busy with skaters during the day. To him, the backdrop of the trees lights dancing off the soft flakes of snow, Ashley, her white faux fur coat - enveloping her. She looked to him like an ice princess, the empty skating rink her court.

Tugging lightly on her fingertips, he spun her until they faced each other. He felt like a peasant, pulling his offering from his pocket, a feeble gesture not measuring up to what he was feeling. "Kaya has helped me not pine for what was. She kept me focused on moving forward, sort of…" Josh paused, fumbling with the small package in his hand as he fought for the words, "You came along and opened up…so much more. I didn't want to wait until tomorrow to give you your present." He handed Ashley the small, neatly wrapped box.

Pausing for a moment, Ashley lifted an eyebrow observing Josh with suspicion. Tugging at the ribbon, she slipped it off of the box. Before opening it, she looked at Josh, who was watching with nervous anticipation that made Ashley giggle a little. Diving into the moment, she pulled the lid off of the small box and revealed a jewelry clamshell. Opening it, she gasped as she looked inside. Holding a hand to her mouth, her eyes studied the present. In the center - a ring. A simple, opalescent sphere rested in the white gold setting. Surrounding the ring was a set of similar spheres, each a different orb-shaped gem.

Snapping her gaze to Josh, she breathed, "Just like the one my father gave me."

Josh's lips pursed in a hopeful grimace.

"I, I can't believe you found this for me."

"Christmas luck, when you were helping me shop for Kaya, I saw it. After I dropped you off, I doubled back to that little shop, the Uncommon…whatever. I had to get it, for you," Josh shrugged.

"It's too much," Ashley argued.

"It's not enough. Not for all that you have given me," Josh replied, his voice firm and even, "I don't think I could begin to let you understand."

Ashley stared at him for a moment, silent and thoughtful. Wrapping her arms around his neck, "I think Kaya said it all." Pushing up on her toes, she pressed her lips against his. In the snow, in the center of town square, as Christmas Eve officially turned to Christmas, they embraced.

Her words hung in his mind. Their conversation, so simple on the surface, resounded in him. The frankness of Kaya's assessment of his mood, the perceptiveness that his daughter had simply by listening to him over the phone, seemed more astute and clear than his own thoughts.

As he leaned against the windowsill, tracing the moonlight on the snow-covered lawn, he thought, maybe Kaya was.

Chapter Twelve

Morning came early in the Daniels house. Sarah and Noah awoke early and were barely contained by Amy, who demanded they wait at least until the coffee was ready. Josh, for one, was very pleased with his sister's demands. He gave each of them a hug as he slogged down the hallway to retrieve his first cup.

When Nick and Bob arose, there was no stopping the children from streaking into the living room to see what Santa had left them. Amidst their squeals and laughter, the adults huddled in the entrance to the room, clinging to their warm mugs as they watched the kids paw through their stockings.

The smell of freshly baked cinnamon rolls began to snake its way throughout the house. Before Josh could fill his second cup of coffee, the doorbell rang. In a flash, his mother dashed by, sprinting to the entry and flung open the door. "Merry Christmas!" she bellowed to their visitor.

"Merry Christmas, Mrs. Daniels. These are for you," Ashley handed Josh's mother a bouquet of flowers arranged with fresh-cut evergreen clippings.

Josh edged by his mother and kissed Ashley on the cheek as he relieved her of two bags.

"Let me get you a cup of coffee!" Josh's mother called, "What do you like in yours? Eggnog, peppermint…"

"Peppermint sounds nice," Ashley agreed and followed Josh into the living room. Josh's father met them in the doorway and gladly received a hug from their guest. "For you, Mr. Daniels. Josh said, you like Pinot."

"You are a fantastic woman. You're welcome in my home anytime, but call me Nick!" the Daniels patriarch grinned.

Flashing him a playful smile, Ashley replied, "Alright, Nick, but be careful what you ask for. I could use a good wine-drinking buddy."

"Ashley!" the kids called out as the leaped up and squeezed past their grandfather to hug her.

"You came for Christmas?" Sarah cried with wide, excited eyes.

"Yep. I have heard so many wonderful things about a Daniels Christmas; I just had to experience it for myself!" Ashley announced, kneeling on the floor next to the kids. Carefully, she pulled the packages from her bags and slid them by the tree with the other presents that seemed to flow from the evergreen like a present avalanche. "I must say, you two must have been very good this year. Are all of those presents for you?"

Puzzled, Noah scratched his head and then announced, "Well, not all of them."

Ashley giggled with the kids as Josh returned with two steaming cups of coffee. The family fully assembled, Ashley addressed the group, "Thank you so much for allowing me to join you today. I feel quite honored to be let into the Daniels family Christmas."

"We're glad to have you," Josh's mother beamed.

"Merry Christmas!" Nick hoisted his cup in the air to a chorus of Merry Christmases, "Well, let's get to the presents!"

Josh and Bob began sorting through the heaping pile and delivering them to the proper recipients. Sarah and Noah inspected each one that was placed beside them the best they could as they waited for all of them to be delivered.

Ashley was surprised to see several presents placed in front of her. "I was hoping I would get to meet whoever put a smile on my little brother's face. I had something squirreled away just in case. And the kids stayed up putting together some things for you as well," Amy explained.

"That is very sweet. I can't wait to see!" Ashley responded.

Soon the living room was carpeted in paper, ribbons, and bows. The kids were tearing wildly into their packages, squealing as they each opened their gifts from Josh. Sarah pulled a Mary Make-over doll from its wrapping while Noah freed a race car set. Each jumped up to give him a hug of thanks. Around the room, the others were equally impressed by Josh's selection.

Amy cast a suspicious look in Ashley's direction, "Josh seems to have done very well this year, are we correct to assume he had a little help?"

"Maybe. He had the stories to create the images of each of you. I simply helped point him in the right direction." Ashley replied modestly.

"You don't like my gift cards and chocolate covered macadamia nuts I usually send?" Josh asked in a mocking puzzled tone.

"We do. We just love the personal touch that we know you have in you, little brother," Amy replied. Her eyes warm and serious, belying her lighthearted tone, "Though the best gift was you coming home."

"Cheers to that!" Ashley said, raising her cup.

Tearing into her presents, she opened a candle set from Amy and two hand-drawn pictures of Ashley and Josh from the children. "Thank you, guys. This is so sweet!" She plopped to the ground and gave each of the kids a hug.

"Your turn, Mr. Josh!" she demanded as she returned to her seat. Hoisting an intricately wrapped box and handing it to him.

Josh carefully loosened the ribbon that held the package together. Pulling the lid off of the box, he slid a heavy object out of tissue paper. Shaking off the tissue, he revealed an ornate snow globe. Inside, a couple skated on an icy pond near a frozen waterfall.

"Not exactly Punch Bowl..." Ashley started.

"It's wonderful," Josh interjected, "I love it.

"I saw it and instantly thought of you. Of us on one blustery day out in the Gorge," Ashley described.

"A day I'll remember always, thank you," Josh planted a kiss on her cheek. Noticing her cup was almost empty, "More coffee?"

"I can get it. Just point me to the kitchen. You stay here with your family," Ashley insisted.

Having found her way, Ashley poured coffee into her cup. Nick appeared behind her, holding up his mug, "Needed a little warm-up myself!" he pronounced. Seeing Amy searching for something to add to her coffee, Nick held up a bottle he had just splashed into his cup, "Irish Cream? Takes the nip out of you!"

"Sure!" Ashley allowed the Daniels elder to top off her cup.

"Nice seeing the life seep back into him," Nick announced, referring to Josh, "You should've seen him when he landed. A miracle if you ask me."

Ashley glowed shyly as she raised her mug, "It is the season."

When the last present was opened, and the kids were busy revisiting their gifts one by one, Bob and Josh started picking up the paper and packaging. Ashley rose to help, but Amy whisked her away, "They can handle it. Come sit and visit." Pulling her to a large sofa occupied by her mom, they sat down.

Within minutes, they were laughing and giggling, learning more about Ashley, and telling tales about Josh growing up. Josh rolled his eyes as his worst fears realized – his mother and sister holding court with his date.

Bob caught his look out of the corner of his eye, "Forget it. You've lost her for hours, might as well relax."

Josh grunted a reply and carried an armful of discarded wrapping into the garage. Knowing Bob was right, Josh returned to plop down with Sarah and Noah, helping them put their new toys together. He tried his best to ignore the tortuous life story that Amy and his mother unveiled to Ashley. His annoyance was compounded when his mother disappeared down the hallway only to return with a load of photo albums.

Page by page, Josh's life flipped through in pictures. From his vantage, Ashley was treated to photos of him in diapers, baseball caps that were too big for him, and tuxes whose styles did not stand the test of time. Overall, hearing the constant laughter, Josh reasoned, was not a bad way to spend Christmas day, even if he was the brunt.

He focused his attention on Noah and Sarah, who thoroughly enjoyed having an adult crawling around with them, playing with their new toys. Even Josh found himself becoming engrossed in saving Sarah's new stuffed baby seal from Noah's laser tag assault.

When the photo tour mercifully ended, Josh had been beaten by Noah's race car three times, and Sarah's fairy princess fashion reached its most elegant glittery form, the family made their way to the dinner table.

Nick stood at the head of the table and addressed the family with his wine glass held high, "Merry Christmas, everyone! As always, having the family together is the best gift of all. This year, we have the additional blessing of having Josh home. No less of a blessing is the wonderful opportunity to meet and share the day with this wonderful young lady, Ashley. Salud!"

"Salud!" they all cheered, toasting their glasses.

"To Kaya. Merry Christmas!" Josh added.

"To Kaya!" the family roared.

After Nick gave the blessing, the family dug into their holiday feast. The table Josh's mother set looked like it could have come from the cover of a holiday magazine. From the giant carved ham, the dishes of deep green, yellow, and orange vegetables to the sparkling holiday glasses that made their presence, but once a year, the meal was as beautiful as it was enticing to eat.

"I haven't had a meal like this in years," Josh commented as he sliced a mouthful of ham.

"Maybe you need to come home more often," his mother said dryly.

To almost everyone's surprise, Josh didn't defend the jab, "Maybe you're right. Thank you for pushing me."

"My pleasure, dear. That's what mothers are for," Carol replied with a devious grin.

"This really is wonderful. It has been a spectacular day. Thank you for including me," Ashley said to the group.

"Are pleasure, especially when we have the opportunity to embarrass and annoy Josh!" Amy grinned.

"What? I loved the stories," Ashley protested, "The highlight of the day."

"There's plenty more. You come by any time!" Carol replied.

"I wish you had time to spend with Kaya. She is truly an amazing child. Little brother did very good," Amy commented.

"I do too. She is very special," Ashley agreed, "I love to see how Josh lights up every time he talks about her."

"He's a great father," Carol claimed.

"You should have seen the coffee shop yesterday. The kids and social workers from the foster group were elated by the generosity and caring that Ashley and her staff shared," Josh said, deflecting the talk away from himself.

"Josh told us about that. That was very nice of you on one of the busiest days to practically shut down for a few hours," Bob said.

"It was worth it. And my customers understood. The shop was slammed afterward, and almost everyone was positive about it," Ashley replied, "You should have seen Josh, though. He was the hit with the kids and the ladies."

"He usually is," Amy quipped.

Ashley suddenly jumped, "Oh my gosh, I almost forgot. Will you please excuse me?"

Pushing back from the table, Ashley streaked out of the room, returning a few moments later. Holding out a folded sheet of paper, she handed it to Josh, "This is from Nella."

Unfolding the construction paper, Josh revealed a crayon scrawled drawing. At the top of the page, a huge star shone over the scene. In the center, a man knelt next to an extremely curly-haired girl, each with their arms reaching out to hug one another. With a deep, introspective sigh, Josh looked up at the group, “This is beautiful.” Passing the picture around to gushes of praise and coos from his family, Josh played once again with the food on his plate.

“See, told you he was a hit. Mrs. Blanchard from the Maplewood Home said Nella was very touched by your attention Josh. She stopped by the shop to thank me last night. Dan came over on his way home and left this with a few thank you notes on my doorstep,” Ashley informed, and excitedly added, “It gets better, Mrs. Blanchard also said that a couple’s paperwork had been approved. It was sitting on her desk when she returned from the shop. Nella spent her first night with her new family last night!”

“I’m glad to hear that. She was very sweet,” Josh replied.

Through the glow of the candles on the table, the scene was picture perfect. His family that he so appreciated, this stunning woman that had delivered him an awakening over the holiday, the news about Nella…the Christmas had been nothing short of magical. He felt incredibly blessed. One thing was missing, a hole that his heart could not ignore – Kaya. As his family and Ashley continued their conversation, Josh’s mind wandered to the phone calls throughout the holiday and seeing Kaya at the church program. She was always so calm and positive. As much as he whined about missing her, she happily told stories of what made her happy, despite the fact that she missed her father very much.

He laughed silently to himself. He could learn a lot from his beautiful little daughter. Picturing her, and her positive smile as she waved goodbye to him last night, she reminded him of someone else—another person who had such a strong, yet calm and positive presence about her. The candle closest to him flickered, softly lighting Ashley's profile. Smiling as always, happily sharing, Josh thought what a beautiful person had come into his life.

When all of the dishes were cleared, Nick was half-snoozing on the sofa, and the kids were once more perusing their gifts, Josh poured two more glasses of wine. Putting on their coats and boots, he and Ashley carried their glasses to the backyard. Josh dusted off two of the swings that were bathed in the glow of the moon.

"It was a great day," he told her, "I'm so glad you came."

Leaning her swing closer to his, she kissed him softly on his lips, "I'm so glad I came."

"You have helped me see so much that I have been missing," he continued, his voice soft, yet confident.

"It can't be easy to break up a family and still find times like this easy on your heart," Ashley defended.

"It's not," Josh admitted, "Every single day that I am not with my daughter kills me. Christmas without her…it's not the same."

Ashley gave a comforting look, "I suppose it's not. But Christmas is still Christmas. It's just different. You got to see her on

Christmas Eve. You get to talk to her and share her experiences as she tells you them. I don't pretend that that's the same, but it has to better than erasing those days altogether."

"It is. That's something that I learned from her…and you this year," Josh nodded his head, "You have given me Christmas back. I don't know how to thank you."

"Hearing you say that is thanks enough," Ashley curved her fingers on his cheek, landing just under his chin, "You are a wonderful man with a wonderful daughter. Shutting yourself away is unfair to the world, especially your family."

"You're right. It just took a steaming hot latte thrown at me to see that," Josh smirked.

"I'm never going to live that down, am I?" Ashley asked, her eyes sparkling in the moon's reflection off of the snow.

"It's funny. I was just thinking how much better Kaya handles all of this than me. She stays so happy, so upbeat. I can genuinely tell she misses me, but she's okay. Reminds me of you. You have such a calm, warm nature about you… so beautiful."

"You have it too, when you aren't burying it, protecting it. You are an intriguing man, Mr. Daniels. You have a kindness that seeps out of you, I think, in spite of yourself sometimes. The way Nella warmed up to you, the way the social workers swooned – oh, they did," she confirmed, a wry, yet wistful look on her face, "The way I had to know more about you."

"You are an angel that helped me to see," Josh said softly.

"You are a wonderful man. You have a terrific family and amazing daughter – all who love you dearly," Ashley said, her look even more pensive, "I love you."

"I love you too."

Setting their wine glasses in the snow, they circled the one another with their arms, their lips closing together. Josh swore he could feel the heat from the moon that brought the blanket of snow to life. He could hear the stars, twinkling like soft Christmas bells. He could feel the empty space in his heart slowly fill. The place with Kaya, as warm and content, as though she were right there with him. He did feel Ashley was an angel. An amazing gift that had been granted him on this magical Christmas.

"Merry Christmas, Daddy!" Kaya's angelic voice sang through the phone.

"Merry Christmas, Kaya. How was your day?" Josh asked.

"It was great. I got some clothes I can only wear here, not exactly island style. I got some new movies to watch on the way home with you too!" Kaya squealed, and her voice became a bit more sullen, "But I miss you, Daddy. Its kind of like Christmas misses something, it's you."

"I know the feeling. I miss you too. Very, very much."

"I asked Mom if you could visit, but I don't think it was her favorite idea. I had a good day anyway. Roger got me some computer games that are supposed to make me smarter, they're okay. I don't feel smarter yet, though," Kaya declared.

"I think you are already brilliant. It would take a lot to improve on that."

"Oh, Daddy," Kaya protested, "You are always my greatest fan."

"Yes, I am. Always will be."

"Did you see Ashley today? I like her. She's very pretty…and nice!"

"Yes, she came over for most of the day. We all had a good time, except when Aunt Amy and your grandmother decided to show her all the pictures of me when I was little," Josh replied.

Kaya giggled, "That would have been funny. I wish I was there to see that! Did you play with my cousins?"

"Yep. Noah and I spent most of the day shooting things with his laser blaster, though we had to have quiet time while Sarah's baby doll was sleeping. They missed you too," Josh declared.

"It would have been nice to have other kids to play with. Maybe next year I can talk Mom into having us all together."

Josh was silent for a moment, trying to imagine that thought, "Maybe."

"Hey, Daddy...," Kaya called.

"Yes?"

"Are you by a window? See those stars? I see them too," Kaya beamed into the phone.

Josh's heart filled like a balloon as he looked up into the clear night sky, "Yes, I do."

"We're never that far apart."

"You're right, sweetheart. We are under the same Christmas stars. No matter where we are, we are close in our hearts," Josh reasoned.

"That sounds kinda corny, but I guess it's true."

Josh laughed, "Alright. So your dad's been a little sentimental lately. Can't help it. I love you."

"I love you too, Daddy."

"Tell your Mom and Roger Merry Christmas for me. Merry Christmas Kaya," Josh said, still leaning against the cold window, staring up at the stars.

"You'll be back for Spring Break?" Ashley asked, her eyes transfixed on kicking the snow off of the footbridge down to the frozen creek below.

"Yes. I can smuggle Kaya out of school a few days early so we can spend some time together before her Mom officially gets her," Josh nodded, his hand grabbing hers, getting her to look at him, "If you are available, I'd love for the three of us share in most of that. Catch the last bit of spring snow on the mountain?"

"I'd love to, but what about your family? They don't get much of a chance to see her either," Ashley asked warily.

"They'll be fine. They are going to see us in Hawaii in February," Josh replied.

"Okay. I have a friend who has a cabin not far from the resort. I'll see if it's free," Ashley suggested.

"Kaya would love that, I would too," Josh grinned, both of his hand in Ashley's now, pulling her directly in front of him, "How about making a trip to Kona? We'd love to show you the island. It is so amazing…" Josh paused for a moment, the picture of this alluring woman sipping a Mai Tai with the Hawaiian sunset behind her, those bright, infectious eyes catching its reflection, that heart-melting smile… "You would love it."

"I'm sure I would…"

"Come on, say yes. I have tons of flyer miles…" Josh urged.

"I can buy a ticket," Ashley defended, "When's a good time to go?"

"When can you get there?" Josh smiled.

Rolling her eyes at his doggedness, she smiled back, leaning in to kiss him. Grabbing his collar, she pulled him in toward her. There was warmth, caring, and passion in their kiss, with just a touch of questioning discomfort which lingered.

Sensing she was feeling the same wonder, he admitted, "I don't know where we are going either. It's okay. All I know is I am incredibly happy when you are with me. I'll take that in any form that makes sense."

"It doesn't have to make sense," Ashley whispered, throwing away her fears and returning to their kiss.

Saying goodbye to his family and Ashley was bittersweet for Josh. He knew that it meant returning to being with his daughter every day; the pain that ripped through his heart would once again be wholly extinguished. Packing up and leaving his parent's home was awkward for Josh. He felt ashamed for having emotionally abandoned them for so long, yet he also felt like he had reconnected with them. They were understanding when he struggled with the tidings of the season and so accepting when he was ready to embrace the holiday. They were just happy he was there, celebrating family and Christmas for their true virtues.

The entire clan made the journey to the airport in two cars just to see Josh and Kaya off. He received huge hugs from Sarah and Noah, whose sad faces tore at Josh as he said his goodbyes. As he said goodbye to Amy, he felt so empowered to have such a confidant in his corner. His sister was a staid beacon in all of the challenging times of his life, letting him find his own way, but always supportive. Aside from Kaya, he knew his sister was his best friend.

As his mother wiped the tears from her cheek, Josh smiled at her, reminding her that they would see them in a little over a month. He couldn't believe he had convinced both his parents and Amy and Bob to plan trips. Promising to send the kids glimpses of their island itinerary, he waved them a final farewell and stepped into the luggage check line.

Worming his way through the post-holiday bustle, Josh found the spot he was to wait for Dana and Kaya. As he watched other travelers make their goodbyes, Josh smiled as he reflected on his trip. Mostly, he thought of the blessing that it was to meet Ashley. If Amy was his lighthouse – a reliable outpost, Ashley was the angel that pulled him from the depth of his wayward journey when he was lost at sea. Completely unaware of his self-imposed sheltered existence and the loss of life that he had sacrificed, the fateful day in the coffee shop was the intervening moment that made his course correct once again.

Instead of feeling lost when Kaya wasn't with him or cast with guilt in enjoyment, he felt like an even better father to her. He felt like a better person. Somehow, by living this respite in parallel made him feel closer to her than when he sulked and stowed himself away from life. He had stories to share with her. He could genuinely hear the happiness in his daughter's voice when she heard he was happy. That made clear sense to him as he felt the same.

For a moment, he began to berate himself for being so foolish for so long, but then decided what had been didn't matter. He was just glad that he finally figured it out. He was especially elated at the help he had received to get there. He could still picture Ashley in his mind, standing on that frozen pond, bundled in her furry white coat, her hair blowing lightly in the breeze, her smile so bright and playful. He pictured her as they talked on the bridge. Preparing to say goodbye was the first glimpse of serious, subjugated expression she had revealed. He thought of her kiss, it felt like a promise, a kiss of hope.

A voice through the crowd caught his ear, and suspended his thoughts. Through the hordes of travelers, one small voice rang to him above all others. Snapping his head in its direction, he saw Kaya, confidently and steadfastly tugging her mother behind her. As she caught sight of her dad, her face brightened. Releasing her mom's hand, she darted through the crowd, weaving her way to Josh. With open arms, she leaped through the air into her father's embrace.

"I missed you so much!" Kaya squealed.

"I missed you too," Josh whispered back, "Ready to go home?"

"Yes!" she answered quickly, only then pausing, "I'll miss Mom and Roger…"

"Of course you will," Josh acknowledged, squeezing Kaya tight. Looking up, he saw the too familiar expression of pain stretching across his ex-wife's face.

Standing up, he walked over to Dana and Roger. Looking directly into Dana's eyes, he said, "I know how that feels. This is the hardest thing either of us has to do." Turning his gaze to Roger, he added, "Kaya told me all of the games that you played with her and how much she enjoyed you. I am glad you are a part of her life now."

"We're all lucky to have her a part of our lives," Roger stated.

"You can't imagine how much I agree with that and more," Josh replied thoughtfully as he scratched his chin, then his eyes widened, "Why don't you guys plan a trip to see us? I know Kaya would get a kick out of showing you guys around the island and share a few of our favorite places."

"Yeah! Come, Mommy! It'll be so much fun," Kaya beamed.

Seriously, please at least say you'll think about it. You can stay with us, or I can squirrel away a week at the resort…," Josh added.

"Sounds good to me," Roger shrugged.

"I…we…we'll say definitely maybe. That's very nice to offer, Josh," Dana replied. And then to Josh's surprise, she reached her arms out to give her ex-husband a big hug, "Happy New Year, Josh. I know you take great care of her. If we can swing it, we'll call you about a trip."

"Please do," Josh insisted, and spinning to Roger held his hand out for a hearty handshake. After Kaya delivered another set of good-bye hugs, they made their way toward the security gate. This time it was Dana who had to bear watching them walk away.

Hand in hand, Josh and Kaya made their way down the terminal. Glancing down, Josh found his daughter bobbing her head cheerfully. Slowly, she drifted closer to her father until she was nudged against his side as they walked. Josh slung his arm around her, pulled her in even tighter, his heart content.

When they found their gate and settled into their seats, Kaya snuggled against her dad. Josh fished an ornately decorated Christmas box from his jacket pocket. "Think you can manage one last present?"

Kaya's eyes grew wide and met with an even wider smile. Taking the package from her father, she gingerly freed the bow from the package. "Did you decorate this, daddy?" Kaya asked with a brow raised in suspicion.

"I had a little help," Josh admitted.

"I thought so, it is very pretty," Kaya conceded. Carefully, she slipped a finger through the taped flaps and slipped the wrapping off, producing a small box. Removing the lid, she found a gleaming charm bracelet. Pulling it from its mooring, she held it up, the pair of attached charms jingling as they dangled in the air. "It's beautiful, daddy! Thank you!" Slinging her arms around her father, she hugged him around his neck.

Releasing her grip, she took a closer look at the pair of charms. The first was a shining heart. On one side of the heart, "KAYA" was inscribed, on the other, "DADDY". The second charm, as brilliant as the first – a star. The symbol that Josh had accepted to tie their individual experiences into their combined shared story.

"Even when we are apart, we are always under the same stars, huh Daddy?" Kaya grinned, staring up at her father.

"Yes, we are," Josh pulled his daughter tight against him, "Yes, we are."

Chapter Thirteen

11 Months Later

Kaya giggled as she raced up the steps. Reaching the landing in front of their door, she stuck her chin in the air, letting the Pacific Breeze blow her hair in the wind, drying what saltwater remained. Behind her, Josh bound up the stairs, his arms wrapped around their boogie boards.

"I could carry one, you know," Ashley protested a few steps below.

"You're on vacation," Josh stated simply.

"I like that. The best tour guide on the island, despite her diminutive age and one fine cabana boy," Ashley grinned, "I guess I can't complain.

Josh set the boards down and fished in his pocket for the keys to the door. He paused, stunned for probably the eleventh time that week by the astonishingly attractive figure on the steps behind him. Ashley looked every part of the beautiful wahine – island woman. Her skin already bronzed from days in the sun. Her wind and saltwater crusted hair transformed the sophisticated beauty of a shop owner to a naturally alluring, playful creature who smiled so contentedly at him. With her tan skin wrapped in a sarong and bikini top, she looked as though she had walked out of the resort's marketing booklet and onto his front porch.

Suddenly, he was whacked back to consciousness by Kaya, who smacked him in the arm and was sternly giving him "stink eye", "You can ogle her later, I gotta go pee!"

Clicking the lock tumblers for his daughter, Kaya burst through and down the hallway. With an enormous smile, Ashley sauntered up to him, "Ogling, huh?" Wrapping her arms around his neck, she looked deeply into his eyes, "I am all yours to ogle. By the way, you're not too shabby to look at yourself island boy." Moving from a deep kiss, she suddenly peeled away, twirled her beach towel, and snapped it at Josh's backside. She paused to take in her beau, clad only in tropical board shorts and flip flops.

"Hey!" he protested, "Don't be starting a war you can't win. Those are native weapons to us!"

"I'll surrender if you fix me one of those Mai Tais…," Ashley shot him her best innocent look, complete with biting her finger as she sashayed her way down the hall. Josh obediently retreated to the kitchen, "I'll meet you on the lanai!"

Josh found her leaning against the rail, the sun on her face, highlighting the amber tones of her and the sun-coaxed freckles that dotted the bridge of her nose. Handing her a freshly crafted Mai Tai, he joined her, leaning his forearms against the rails of the lanai, his bottle of lime-infused Longboard swirling over the edge of the balcony. For several moments, they enjoyed the dramatic view and the ocean breezes. The only sounds were the waves breaking and the occasional cooing of a Kolea bird wintering in the islands.

"I love it here, it truly is beautiful," Ashley said, her gaze still fixed on the ever-rolling Pacific, "I can see why you chose to move here.

Josh grinned at her, "It is a magical place. I remember the first time I came here. It was like I was a different person, all of the usual stresses and chaos of life on the mainland seemed to melt away. Still ambitious, still plenty of bills to be paid, just a calm overtaken me that I could manage it all in stride and perspective."

"I can see that. It's the "aloha", right?"

"Part of it. It's aloha, ohana...work hard for what is truly important," Josh's eyes glanced inside the condo and towards Kaya.

"Kaya said it was the first time since you the divorce that you decorated for Christmas. I'm proud of you, Mr. Scrooge," Ashley half teased.

Josh plucked a purple orchid he had garnished Ashley's Mai Tai with and gently slid it into her hair behind her ear. "An amazing angel bestowed a gift to me, oh…about a year ago."

"Oh, an angel, really? And just how did she do that?" Ashley raised a single brow.

"Well, she first caught my attention by tossing hot coffee at me. When that didn't work, she charmed me. Dragging me to enchanting places, showing me beautiful things," Josh illuminated. Now they were looking into each other's eyes instead of the ocean.

"Like frozen waterfalls and children skating?"

"Yes. But so much more," Josh leaned in closer to her, his hand stroking the hair near where he placed the orchid, "She showed me that Christmas didn't stop when you couldn't be with the ones you love. That there was still a lot to be shared under the Christmas star."

"Sounds angelic."

"It's more than that," Josh swallowed hard, "She showed me that I could love again."

Ashley opened her mouth to quip back, but instead, leaned into his kiss. "I hope she taught you that you deserve to be loved," she draped her arms around his neck.

They enjoyed the closeness in silence. Enjoying the sun's warmth, the scents of plumeria and sea air, they danced to their own silent music, oblivious to the world around them.

"Ahhhem!" Kaya cleared her throat as she stepped out onto the balcony.

Josh swung one of his arms free and held it out towards his daughter, "You can get in on this, plenty of love here."

Kaya stepped into a double hug, closing the open loop on one side of Josh and Ashley. "Do we have to leave, Daddy?" she asked sullenly from within their group hug.

"Yes, Kaya, your mom misses you."

In a pouty voice, Kaya relented, "I know, I miss her too. It's just…just I love the island."

Ruffling her hair with his hand, "And it loves you. Hey, how about an early present?" Josh raised his eyebrows to a vehemently nodding Kaya. Bolting through the lanai door, he vanished into the cond.

Kaya shot Ashley a quizzical look only to be met with a grin and a shrug. She didn't have to wait long, as Josh burst onto the lanai as quickly as he had left it. In his hand, he held out a small box wrapped in silver paper with jacquard palm trees shining in the sun's rays.

Plucking off a tiny metallic bow, Kaya tore at the paper. In seconds, she had revealed a blue box, after an anxious glance towards her father, she tilted up the lid. Inside were two shining charms: a palm tree and flip flop. Excitedly, Kaya freed them from her moorings and held her wrist out for her dad to attach them to her charm bracelet.

"They're beautiful, Daddy!" Kaya said, admiring her present.

"We had some of our best times here. They're not much, but now you can carry a little bit of Hawaii with you," Josh replied, giving his daughter a squeeze.

"I still wish we could stay…," Kaya sulked, casting her gaze at the late afternoon sets that were rolling into shore

"I know. But there are so many people looking forward to us being there," Josh consoled and then offered a twisted grin, "Besides, we can't miss the first-ever multi-family mixed holiday. Now that will be exciting."

"I still can't believe Mom agreed to that. What did you do to her and Roger when they came, and I wasn't with you?" Kaya looked at her father with impish suspicion.

"The magic of the islands. What I can't figure out is how I agreed to live back on the mainland. I think everyone should have just moved here," Josh said hopefully.

"I could run the coffee shop from here. Maybe buy a coffee plantation and send my own stuff," Ashley agreed.

"Don't tease me," Josh groaned, "I had a good thing going with my little life selling timeshares and surfing with Kaya. But the look in Dana's eyes when she had to say goodbye. I know that pain, no parent should be away from their child."

"Who's the angel after all?" Ashley asked.

Before Josh could respond, Kaya wrapped her arms around his waist and looked up into her dad's eyes, "My daddy."